"Come to my room, Martine."

Bruno said the words with an urgency that made her stiffen.

She turned on him, her face white now. "I feel sick, do you know that? You got me drunk, you knew I wasn't used to drinking, and you kept pouring wine into me, right the way through dinner. You had this in mind all the time, didn't you? You set me up, and it nearly worked. I almost fell for the oldest trick in the book."

There was a silence you could have cut with a knife. His eyes turned to glittering black ice. "You did fall for it. You're so frustrated that you fell into my hands like a ripe peach, and I didn't even have to try very hard...."

CHARLOTTE LAMB was born in London in time for World War II, and spent most of it moving from relative to relative to escape bombing. Educated at a convent, she married a journalist, and now has five children. The family lives on the Isle of Man. Charlotte Lamb has written over a hundred books.

Books by Charlotte Lamb

ISBN 0-373-11733-7

BODY AND SOUL

Copyright © 1994 by Charlotte Lamb.

First North American Publication 1995.

CHARLOTTE LAMB

Body and Soul

Harlequin Books

TORONTO • NEW YORK • LONDON
AMSTERDAM • PARIS • SYDNEY • HAMBURG
STOCKHOLM • ATHENS • TOKYO • MILAN
MADRID • WARSAW • BUDAPEST • AUCKLAND

CHAPTER ONE

MARTINE was late, and in a hurry, so she leapt out of her taxi and ran across the pavement towards the Mayfair restaurant, too intent to notice the man in evening dress who got out of a parked car on the other side of the road and headed in the same direction.

There was a moment when either of them could have held back, but, although they glanced briefly at each other, neither of them stopped. Martine thought she was nearer and would get there first; but he moved faster.

They collided in the revolving door. Which promptly jammed—with them crushed together inside one section. Martine looked up, her eyes as stormily green as northern seas. The eyes that met hers were black, cold, irritated.

'If you back out, that will free the door!' said a deep, dark voice with a faint foreign accent which she couldn't identify.

'If you had had the manners to let me go first this wouldn't have happened! *You* step back!' she snapped.

It was all his fault, and Martine didn't like his peremptory tone, or the fact that she had been forced so close to him. You couldn't have got a sheet of paper between them, in fact—which meant that his body actually touched hers, making her very aware of his powerful build. He might be wearing civilised evening dress but underneath it was a distinctly primitive body: six feet of muscle and bone and smooth, tanned skin, a face that could have been carved out of granite.

'There's no point in arguing about whose fault it is!' he bit out. 'Just wriggle backwards.'

'Any wriggling can be done by you,' Martine informed him.

Just because she was almost a foot shorter than him, fine-boned and slender, he needn't imagine that she was a helpless female and a pushover. She wasn't backing down, even if it meant they stayed jammed in this door all night.

He stared down into her angry green eyes, and she bristled like a cat faced with danger, the hair standing up on the back of her neck.

Something about the arrogant tilt of his head, the sleek black hair, the cool eyes, reminded her of a man she had once loved, but who had walked out on her to marry a girl with rich parents. Three years had gone by since then, and Martine had dated other men, but never fallen in love like that again, and never meant to. She had been badly hurt once. She didn't intend to repeat the experience.

'Look, even an idiot should see that the easiest way of freeing the door would be for you to back out,' he coldly pointed out.

'Oh, very well,' Martine said, shifting sideways to get into a better position for wriggling out. His foot was in the way. Her elegant little black shoes had thin, high heels, like stilettos. She felt one of them sink into the top of his polished shoe.

He started violently, took a sharp breath, and said something under that breath which she couldn't quite hear but which sounded suspiciously like swearing.

'Sorry,' she said, and met glittering black eyes.

'You did that deliberately!' he accused.

'Don't be ridiculous! I was simply trying to get out. How was I to know you would put your foot in the way?'

He eyed her with dislike. His nostrils flared, a white line of rage around his mouth.

'I suppose I'll have to get us out of here or we'll be here all night,' he muttered. 'Just stand still, will you?'

Turning sideways, he began to slide past her, his body pressing against hers in the process, his long thigh pushing past, his arm brushing her breast. Despite herself she felt a sharp needle of sexual awareness stab through her and tensed in shock.

'Hey! Watch it!' she hissed, guessing that he was inflicting his intimacy on her deliberately in male revenge because she hadn't been the one to back out.

It was a mistake to say anything. It made him stop, dead, looking down at her with those dark, narrowed eyes barely inches above her own, their bodies still touching. 'Don't flatter yourself,' he said through his teeth. 'This isn't giving me any thrill at all, I assure you.'

Martine reddened crossly. 'Oh, just get a move on, will you?' she muttered. 'We're attracting a crowd!'

There were people on the inside of the restaurant, trying to get out, and another couple on the pavement, trying to get in, all watching them and grinning. They were providing live entertainment and Martine felt very silly and very angry. She hid it, giving their audience helpless smiles and shrugs.

Her reluctant companion finally squeezed out backwards, and Martine immediately pushed the revolving door to emerge in the restaurant, murmured an apology to the people waiting, slid out of her silk evening jacket and handed it to a hovering waiter.

'Is Mr Redmond here, yet?'

'If he is, he'll be in the bar, miss.'

Behind her she heard the revolving door turning and was aware of a looming presence emerging.

She ignored him.

As she walked into the circular, discreetly lit bar, she saw a faint reflection swimming in the black glass lining the wall behind the bar counter. First herself, slender, in black georgette, her face thrown into odd prominence, a pale, shimmering oval, her neck long and slim, a white magnolia pinned just above her breasts, at the edge of her deep neckline, her dark auburn hair coiled low on her nape; and, walking behind her, a head taller than her, the black-haired foreigner in his stiff white shirt front and black jacket.

She had to admit they made an interesting composition in black and white; the only colour visible was the dark flame of her red hair.

She halted to look around the room. There were a few people in the bar, but there was no sign of Charles, which didn't surprise her. He was often unpunctual, but then he had so much on his mind. Since the death of his wife he had buried himself in work; sometimes he didn't seem quite sure which day of the week it was! She only hoped he would remember that he had asked her to have dinner here tonight.

He had just flown back from New York that morning and hadn't been in to the office since landing; had stayed at home, resting after the trip.

He had made their date for tonight from New York. No doubt he wanted to talk to her out of the office; there was always too much going on there for any possibility of a private conversation, and since much of the information he needed to give her was very confidential they chose their meeting-places carefully.

She sat down at one of the empty tables. Immediately a waiter came over. 'What will you have to drink, madam?'

'Oh . . . just a glass of sparkling mineral water, please,' she said, crossed one slender, shapely leg over the other, her fine, filmy skirt riding up a little so that she had to stroke it down over her knee. Casually glancing around the bar, she found herself looking into black eyes on the other side of the room, eyes that had been watching her smoothing down her skirt, had coldly assessed her legs, risen to give the same unimpressed speculation to her figure and face.

Martine gave him a glacial stare back. She never liked getting looks like that—as if she were an object, not a human being. Some men used it as a silent insult. She had the feeling this one did, especially remembering the way he had spoken to her while they were jammed in the revolving door.

He calmly detached his gaze, looked down, shot his cuff back to allow a glimpse of his gold wristwatch and frowned, then got to his feet. Martine stiffened, thinking for a few seconds that he was coming over here to her table.

Instead he walked out of the bar without giving her another look. Several women in the room watched him avidly.

OK, he had his points, especially when you saw him in a good light, thought Martine. She liked tall men, especially when they moved like that. The tan was striking, too. He probably stripped well; his body had interesting proportions: broad shoulders, slim hips, long, long legs.

Catching herself up, she grimaced. What was she thinking about? Men like him were nothing but a disaster. She hadn't had a man in her life for almost a year, that was the trouble, and however hard she worked, however many hours she put into her job, she still felt pretty blue at times. Frustration and loneliness must be having a dire effect on her brains for her to look twice at that guy, though!

She crossly took a couple of salted almonds from the bowl in the middle of the table and popped them into her mouth while she, too, consulted her watch.

Where was Charles?

She had no sooner thought the question than she saw him hurrying towards her, a thin, slight, fair man in a well-cut dark suit.

'Sorry,' he apologised, sliding into the seat next to her. 'Am I late, or were you early?'

'I've only been here a moment,' she lied, smiling at him, her eyes faintly anxious as she absorbed the air of weariness he habitually wore. She hadn't seen him for a week and was struck by the way he was ageing. He was only forty-five, but he looked older; there were lines around his mouth and eyes, his skin had a grey tinge.

The waiter brought her drink, looked at Charles expectantly.

'My usual, Jimmy,' Charles told him with a smile.

'Yes, Mr Redmond,' said the waiter, beaming, pleased because Charles had remembered his name.

Charles ate here frequently. He lived in a luxurious penthouse flat a short walk away; this was his nearest local restaurant and he liked the place. He had a married couple who ran his home. Mr Wright was his chauffeur and handyman, and looked after his clothes; Mrs Wright cleaned and cooked in the flat. But Charles let them have three evenings a week free, and came here to eat.

The waiter walked away and Charles turned back to smile at Martine.

'That's my favourite dress, you always look lovely in it,' he said, and a faint flush crept into her face. She had put on the black georgette because whenever she wore it Charles told her how much he liked it.

Working for him meant a constant succession of important social gatherings for which she required a large and very expensive wardrobe, so she had plenty of clothes to choose from. She got a special allowance for clothes and Charles encouraged her to buy from good designers because as his personal assistant she was always representing the bank and Charles felt she should look expensive and elegant at all times. It was the image he wished the bank to convey: moneyed, sophisticated, cool.

'Thank you, Charles, you look very elegant yourself tonight,' she murmured, and he gave her a rueful little quirk of the mouth.

'Why, thank you.' He didn't sound convinced. No doubt he knew his suit no longer fitted perfectly, revealed how thin he was getting, emphasised the fact that he had lost even more weight since she last saw him.

Charles had never been heavily built, but after his wife's death two years ago he had lost weight as if his flesh was melting away. That hadn't been the only change in him. His hair had been a lovely pale gold; the shock of Elizabeth's death had left him with a sprinkling of silver hairs and a haunted look in his blue eyes.

He had been driving and had emerged unscathed himself with a few minor bruises and cuts and a slight head injury. Elizabeth had been killed instantly; Charles had never quite got over it. He blamed himself and was guilty because he had not died too. If they had had children it might have been easier for him to recover from the shock, but he and Elizabeth hadn't yet got around to a family.

'Thanks, Jimmy,' he told the waiter as the man appeared with a double whisky and soda on a silver tray. 'I'm expecting another guest to join us—would you keep an eye open for him? His name's Falcucci, Bruno Falcucci.'

'An Italian gentleman, would he be, sir? There's a gentleman making a telephone call in the foyer who's talking in Italian. I'll check if it's Mr Falcucci, shall I?'

'Thanks, Jimmy,' Charles said, smiling at him again.

Ice clinked in the glass as Charles took a swallow of whisky.

'Who's joining us?' Martine asked, faintly disappointed because she had been looking forward to dinner alone with him, but not taken entirely by surprise because Charles often used social occasions to smooth a business deal, and she was frequently included in the party, whether it was lunch or dinner or a cocktail party.

'A cousin of mine,' Charles said with a glint of mischief in his blue eyes.

As startled as he had obviously expected her to be, Martine said, 'You've never mentioned having any close relatives.'

Charles had, from time to time, told her something about himself and his background, and other members of staff at the bank had dropped the odd crumb of gossip. She had gained the impression that Charles had no near family, and very few close friends. He had always been so wrapped up in his work, even while his wife was alive, and since her death he had cut his social life almost to nil.

His friends were largely colleagues or business acquaintances, most of them married, with family commitments, making Charles an odd man out on most social occasions. That was why he had fallen into the habit lately of taking Martine along with him to any private gathering to which he was invited.

They weren't romantically involved, simply very good friends as well as close colleagues; it suited them both to have an escort for an evening now and then, and they were both deeply involved in their work.

Charles had told her that he had been an after-thought by his parents, both of whom, apparently, had been in their late forties when he was born, their first and only child, a much loved and indulged one. Perhaps having old parents had made him so serious, so tied to duty and work?

They had died long ago, when he was a young man, leaving Charles an enormous fortune and the major interest in the family merchant bank. Charles had once said that he had begun to work as soon as he left university, and hadn't noticed much about the world outside banking until he was nearly forty himself. That year he had been in Paris at an international conference and met a beautiful French model half his age, Elizabeth, raven-haired, tiny, exquisite. Charles fell like a ton of bricks, married her just weeks later, only to lose her again within two years, a tragedy which made him, for Martine, a deeply romantic, star-crossed figure.

She felt highly protective towards Charles, as well as liking him.

'Bruno is the only close relative I have,' Charles said now, giving her a smiling, rueful shrug. 'And I've only met him a couple of times; he lives in Switzerland.'

'Switzerland? And he's in banking, of course,' she said with a wry expression.

Charles looked amused suddenly. 'You think that follows naturally? Well, you're right, he is in banking, I suppose it was in his genes. Or perhaps his mother talked him into joining a bank? Anyway, he works for the Swiss Bank Corporation at the moment, but tonight I intend to ask him to join us.'

Martine's green eyes widened. 'Oh, I see.' Now what did that mean? she wondered, startled.

Charles went on quietly, 'I don't want anyone else to know this, Martine; I'm telling you because I trust you completely. I want you to know, I've just made a new will, leaving my shares in the bank to him. There's nobody else for me to leave them to.'

Martine felt cold suddenly. 'You're talking as if...good heavens, you're only forty-odd. You'll marry again, Charles. Oh, I know you still miss Elizabeth, and it isn't easy to get over things like that, but you sound as if you've given up on life, and you mustn't! There's plenty of time to think about making wills!'

Charles gave a faint, wry smile. 'After working in banking for years, Martine, I'd have thought you knew better than that! It is never wise to put off making a will.'

Frowning, she shrugged. 'In principle, no, but...'

'In practice, too. You should make one yourself. One never knows what's around the next corner.' His blue eyes had that haunted look again; he was thinking about Elizabeth and that crash.

Martine put a hand on his arm, comforting silently, and he gave her a quick, crooked smile, coming back to the present moment.

'Anyway, I've made my will. Actually, Bruno should have had shares in the bank long ago; his mother was my father's only sister! But my grandfather refused to leave anything at all to his daughter, Una, because she married against his will—a Swiss doctor she met on a holiday at Lake Como. Her parents disapproved violently. First, Frederick was a foreigner, and secondly he was not in banking. Worst of all, he had very little money, but he was apparently a delightful man, a good man and a good doctor. Una was very happy with him, but her father never forgave her for marrying him, so he left all his money to my father.'

'That does seem unfair,' Martine agreed. 'It must have made your aunt very unhappy.'

'I'm sure it did.'

'And it led to a family feud!' Martine murmured, and Charles laughed.

'You have a disconcerting streak of romanticism!'

She blushed. She always tried to hide it; it didn't go down well in banking circles, for one thing, and, for another, it had led her into a painful love-affair and left her with a broken heart and bitter disillusion.

'I suppose it was something along those lines, though,' Charles shrugged. 'My parents exchanged

Christmas cards with Aunt Una but they never visited Switzerland, and Aunt Una never came back to England. This big gulf opened up between them.'

'How sad!' It seemed pretty childish to Martine, but the things people did to each other often were, she thought.

Charles sighed. 'It is really, isn't it? Sad and very stupid. When my parents died I lost contact with Aunt Una altogether, but she died a few years ago, and Bruno wrote to tell me. I happened to be going to Switzerland on that banking commission tour so I looked him up while I was there, and I liked him.'

'Does he know you've made him your main beneficiary?' Martine shrewdly asked.

Charles gave her an amused look. 'Not yet.'

Martine's eyes narrowed speculatively. This Bruno Falcucci might not know yet that Charles had left the Redmond share of the bank to him, but he would know that Charles was unmarried and had no other heir, and, if he was shrewd, as he probably was if he was a senior bank executive, he would probably have worked out that he had a chance of persuading Charles to leave him some money.

'Did you invite him to come to London, or is he here off his own bat?'

'He rang me last week to say he had to come to London on business,' Charles informed her, still looking amused. 'What a suspicious little mind you've got!'

'I didn't say a word!'

'You don't need to! I can read your thoughts— after all, I know you very well, Martine.' He looked down into her green eyes and they exchanged an intimate, laughing look.

At that instant somebody strolled up to the table and Charles glanced round, exclaimed, stood up, holding out his hand, his drawn and tired face lighting up.

'Ah, there you are, Bruno! I was beginning to think you had forgotten all about tonight!'

'I've been looking forward to the evening all week,' a deep, cool voice drawled.

Martine sat there transfixed, her mouth open and her nerves in shreds. It would be him, wouldn't it?

Of all the men in the world, she had had to pick on Bruno Falcucci to take an instant dislike to! It hadn't occurred to her for an instant that the man she had got stuck in the revolving door with might be the man she and Charles were waiting for.

Charles was smiling, gesturing to include her in the circle. 'Bruno, I want you to meet my right hand—Martine Archer, my personal assistant for the last four years.'

Martine numbly held out her hand.

Bruno Falcucci took it, his powerful tanned fingers swallowing up her small, pale ones.

She risked a glance upwards. His black eyes coldly mocked her. He said something polite and distant. She answered with equal remoteness. He released her hand.

'Sit down, have a drink; their whisky is very good,' Charles told him.

'I don't drink spirits.' He looked at Martine's glass. 'Is that mineral water? I'll have the same, thank you.'

'I'd forgotten you don't drink,' Charles said, made a face.

'Like your assistant here, I like to keep a cool head,' Bruno Falcucci drawled, and Martine gave him a flicking glance. Oh, very funny! she thought.

Charles ordered the drink, adding, 'And bring the menus, Jimmy, will you? Now, Bruno, what sort of business brings you to London?'

'Banking,' the answer smoothly came.

Charles laughed. 'Of course. Is it confidential? Shall we change the subject?'

'I can't talk in detail about it, I'm afraid. You may read about it in the financial Press some time, but not yet.'

'Well, how long do you plan to stay? Can you tell us that?'

'A week, maybe two. Then I might take a holiday—fly on to Greece, perhaps, or even as far as the Caribbean. I want to relax for a while, unwind, get some sun before I go back to work.'

'You have an amazing tan already!' said Charles. 'Don't you think so, Martine?'

She gave another brief glance in Bruno Falcucci's direction; let her lids droop indifferently over her eyes again. 'Amazing,' she said offhandedly.

She felt Bruno looking at her closely, considering her rich auburn hair, the fine-boned face with the warm, curved mouth and fierce green eyes, before running his gaze down over her body in arrogant appraisal.

Her flush deepened and she felt the back of her neck prickle.

'Where do you go for a holiday?' he asked her.

She shrugged, reluctant to answer.

'Oh, Martine doesn't like hot countries,' Charles answered for her. 'Like most redheads, her wonderful skin doesn't like too much sun. But we had a terrific time in Sweden last summer, didn't we, Martine? And Switzerland was fun a couple of years ago.'

'Especially the *après-ski*, no doubt,' Bruno drawled.

He was making no attempt to hide what he was thinking, his gaze flicking from her to Charles and back again, glinting with cynicism.

He suspected her of having an affair with Charles, she realised. He couldn't be serious! Charles was almost old enough to be her father!

Oh, he was still very good-looking in a weary way, but he had no energy, his hair was thinning and turning silver, his elegant, fine-cut features had a distinct look of strain. She was deeply fond of Charles, she felt sorry for him; but that was all. She resented Bruno Falcucci's speculative stare, the cool cynicism in his eyes.

The head waiter arrived. 'Have you chosen yet, sir?' he asked Charles, who looked at the others.

'I'm ready to order—how about you two?'

Martine nodded. So did Bruno.

She chose melon and sole with a salad; Bruno chose melon, too, with prosciutto, followed by a steak, also with a salad; and Charles ordered melon followed by an omelette with a salad. He ate almost nothing these days. He would probably just pick at his food.

While they waited to be told their table was ready Charles and Bruno talked about the international banking situation. Martine listened intently, absorbing with a faint dismay the fact of Bruno Falcucci's swift, hard intelligence. Charles knew what he was talking about, but he was like a machine running on half-power lately—he kept fading, losing interest, missing vital points. She began to suspect that Bruno could run rings around him.

There was no doubt about it. The man was potentially lethal. And she had a sinking feeling that Charles wouldn't listen if she tried to warn him, would just laugh at her.

The head waiter came back, smiling. 'Whenever you're ready, Mr Redmond...'

'Shall we go in?' suggested Charles, rising. Martine got to her feet. He put a hand under her arm in a gallant gesture, to which she submitted, smiling at him, her eyes affectionate. He was always chivalrous, an old-fashioned man in many ways; she liked that.

Out of the corner of her eye, she caught sight of Bruno Falcucci's face: jet eyes watching her with sardonic amusement, mouth wry. Martine's smile stiffened into anger. It was going to be an ordeal to sit through a meal with that man across the table. She wished she couldn't read his mind so clearly, but it was as if his thoughts leapt across the table to her—or maybe he was actually allowing her, or willing her, to pick up what he was thinking!

Yet why should he? She frowned, letting Charles steer her into the dining-room. Her imagination was really working overtime, surely? She was building Bruno Falcucci up into some sort of bogeyman!

She was seated between the two men at the table, but from then on she turned all her attention, and her body, towards Charles, practically ignoring the other man except when she had no option.

Bruno Falcucci leaned back in his chair, a brooding presence, watching her out of narrowed eyes, physically dominating the circle they made: herself, Charles and him, around this table, with his wide black-clad shoulders, his deep chest and hard face.

Charles dominated the talking, though, and was too absorbed in his favourite subject, international finance, to be aware of the silent duel going on across the white-damask-covered table with its spray of dark red roses in the centre. The dining-room was shadowy, and a softly shaded lamp gave them exactly enough light in which the table glittered with crystal glass, silver cutlery and fine bone china and their faces glowed, now in shadow, now in light, like shifting masks.

It was towards the end of the meal that Charles finally asked Bruno Falcucci the question Martine knew he had been planning to put to him.

'How would you feel about leaving your present job, Bruno, and coming to work for us in a rather more senior position?'

If Bruno was surprised he didn't show it. There was a beat of time when he just sat there, as if absorbing the possibilities, then he calmly said, 'That's a very flattering offer, Charles. I would need to know precisely what you had in mind, of course, and I'd need time to think it over, but in principle I'm certainly interested.'

Charles beamed. 'I hoped you would be. You wouldn't regret the decision if you accepted, Bruno, I promise you that. You could have a splendid future with us, far more exciting than anything you have in prospect at the moment. Ours is a family bank and you are my only male relative.'

He shouldn't be stating the situation quite so frankly. He was betraying the weakness of his position, Martine thought, watching Bruno Falcucci closely, her green eyes sharp and hostile.

He was watching Charles, and his face was a polite mask. Martine would have given a good deal to know what he was thinking, whether he was excited, triumphant, elated. He gave no clues.

'I'll get Martine to put together a proposition for you, setting out all the terms,' Charles promised as he called for the bill. 'And after you've had time to digest the contents, we can talk it over. I'm going to be frank with you—I think your mother should have been provided for in her father's will; she should have had shares in the bank.'

Bruno nodded. 'She should.'

There was a ruthless set to his jaw, the spark of anger in his black eyes. If Charles thought Bruno did not resent the way his mother had been treated, he was clearly wrong. Bruno resented it bitterly. Martine shivered. She hoped Charles hadn't made a fatal mistake. Yet what threat could Bruno present to him? Charles owned a majority of the shares in the bank; Bruno couldn't hurt him.

Charles smiled at him, apparently blithely unaware of the dark feeling in the younger man. 'I want to make up for the past, Bruno. I want you in the family business, where you belong.'

Martine shifted restlessly, frowning. Haven't you got eyes? she wanted to ask Charles. Can't you see what he's like under the good looks and the formal good manners?

Bruno flicked one of those brief, cold glances her way. Charles might not be picking up her agitation, but Bruno Falcucci was, and her dismay didn't bother him. He looked into her eyes, then away, one black brow curling sardonically.

A hard spot of red burnt in her cheeks. She knew what that lifted eyebrow had said. She might oppose him but she wouldn't be a problem, he could deal with her.

Well, that was what he thought! They would see about that.

Charles signed the bill, folded some notes into the leather wallet in which the bill had arrived, and stood up, yawning, looking suddenly drained and white.

'I'm sorry, Martine,' he said in a wearily apologetic voice. 'I'd planned to drive you home myself, but I'm barely able to stay on my feet—will you be very cross if I just put you into a taxi back to Chelsea?'

'Don't worry about it,' she began, but Bruno interrupted.

'I have my car parked outside; I'll drop her off.'

'I thought you said you were staying at the Savoy? There's no need to drive out to Chelsea, I can easily get a taxi.' Martine certainly didn't want him driving her home. The very idea of being alone with the man even for five minutes sent shivers down her spine.

'It's still early. I would enjoy a drive along the river,' he shrugged.

Charles beamed. 'And you can get to know each other! That's a wonderful idea, I should have thought of it myself. Martine is indispensable to me, Bruno. She can tell you all you need to know about the way the bank runs.'

His car was parked across the street. As he began to walk towards it Martine caught Bruno Falcucci's secret smile, and tensed. If she hadn't known how it would upset Charles she would have slapped his face.

Turning away, she walked with Charles to his car, watching him with concern.

'You look quite ill, Charles. You've been working too hard for far too long. I think you need a long holiday. Why don't you take a few days off work and get away?'

'I will, soon,' he said quietly, bent and kissed her cheek. 'You're my guardian angel—don't think I'm not aware of it. Now, be nice to Bruno. I want him to join us, Martine, sell the bank to him. I've done some quiet research on him and he has quite a record, he's pulled off some brilliant deals. Even if he wasn't family, I'd want him, but as he is a Redmond, even though his name is different, I'm determined to get him by hook or by crook.'

'Well, in that case I'll do what I can,' she promised as Charles got behind the wheel of his silver Rolls. She meant what she said, despite her private reservations about the man. She would certainly sell the bank to Bruno Falcucci, but she doubted if it would be necessary. She had the feeling no persuasion would be required to get him to join them. He had always planned to do so.

Charles smiled at her through the window as he started the softly purring engine.

'I know I can always trust you. Goodnight, Martine, see you tomorrow.'

He drove off and she turned to find Bruno Falcucci right behind her, lounging against a long, sleek, vintage black Rolls-Bentley. It was one of the loveliest cars she had ever seen; her mouth watered at the sight of it. She loved old cars.

He opened the passenger door, his body graceful as he held the door for her. 'Where am I to take you?'

'Do you know Chelsea?' she curtly asked, having already discovered that he had been to London a number of times.

He nodded. 'Vaguely. I make for Parliament Square and head off along the Embankment, right?'

She nodded. 'I live a stone's throw from the Tate Gallery, I'll guide you after we get to Millbank.'

She slid into the Bentley's interior, instinctively stroking the soft, pale cream leather seats, giving the dashboard an appreciative inspection.

'Is this yours, or have you borrowed or hired it?' she asked as Bruno got in beside her.

His tanned hands lightly holding the wheel he turned his black head and gave her a long, cool look.

'It's mine. I just bought it.'

It must have cost a fortune; she wondered how much he earned a year to be able to afford a toy like this. Well, she would find out soon, when he and Charles began negotiations.

'You aren't married, Mr Falcucci?'

He shook his head, that sardonic smile in evidence again.

'Have you ever been?' she asked.

'No, have you?'

'No,' she said tersely.

'You're a devoted secretary, though,' he drawled. 'Lucky Charles.'

He turned his head again, deliberately, to meet her stare and Martine let all her dislike and distrust of him show in her face.

'If you hurt Charles in any way I'll kill you!' she told him.

His brows shot up and he gave her that cool, sardonic smile, then took her breath away by what he said next.

'If he was going to marry you, he'd have done so long ago, you know. You're wasting your time waiting for him; which seems a pity, looking the way you do.' His dark eyes flicked down over her body and a wave of heat flowed through her. Softly he added, 'I'm sure a lot of men would be only too happy to help you forget Charles. I might even volunteer myself!'

Martine went dark red, her hands clenching, her teeth together, but she refused to play his game by answering or defending herself, explaining that he was wrong. Information was power, Charles had taught her long ago. Never give it away, use it for your own purposes and do so sparingly. So she let Bruno Falcucci imagine that he had hit on the truth, just gave him one icy glance, then said in a tight, brusque voice, 'Take the next turn on the right, would you?'

The Bentley spun round the corner and began moving along the wide street of rather stately Victorian houses.

'No comment, then?' Bruno Falcucci asked her, watching her out of the corner of his eyes.

'Stop here, please,' was all Martine said.

He braked and turned towards her but she was already getting out of the car. She slammed the door then bent towards the window and he leaned over to wind it down to hear what she said.

Martine looked into his gleaming, dark eyes. 'Remember, if you hurt Charles, I'll make sure you pay for it,' she said, then turned on her heel and walked away.

CHAPTER TWO

'YOU have to admit,' said Annie, one of the share
analysts, some months later, 'he's an asset to the
bank!'

'Oh, please, no puns this early in the morning!'
winced Martine.

'You've got no sense of humour where he's concerned, that's the trouble,' complained Annie, who
was a year younger, and very pretty: small, fair,
bubbly, and very popular with the men. 'And
you've dodged my question! He's the hottest thing
we've acquired in years. Look at that Ambleham-
Tring merger—I hear we've picked up a lot more
business from that, and his client list has doubled
since he arrived.'

'Haven't you got any work to do?' Martine was
staring at her VDU, frowning over the string of figures coming up. 'Because if you haven't, I have.
With Charles ringing in to say he's working at home
today, and our trip to Rome starting tomorrow, I've
got so much to do I'll be working until very late
tonight, so get off my desk and go away, Annie!'

'In a minute,' Annie said, wriggling like a child
on the edge of the desk, her small feet swinging
back and forth. 'I wanted to ask you something . . .'

'Well, what?' Martine irritably asked,
wondering how Annie could be so thick-skinned.
What did you have to do to get rid of her?

'Has he got a woman tucked away somewhere? I mean, he hasn't dated anyone since he joined us, he says he isn't married, and I can't believe he's gay, so is there someone in the background?'

'I don't know, I don't care, and will you please shut up about Bruno Falcucci, get off my desk and let me get on with my work?' Martine frequently wished she had never heard the man's name, let alone met him. He had been here nearly four months and she sometimes felt as if the whole place revolved around him. It certainly did as far as the female staff were concerned. They couldn't stop talking about him; half of them were in love with him and the others were simply fascinated.

Except Martine, of course. If anything, she disliked him more now than she had the first day she'd met him.

She had watched grimly while he became a director and immediately began to dominate board meetings, making himself the centre of power on the board, a voice to be reckoned with, pushing Charles further and further out of the picture.

It was what she had feared from the beginning, but Charles would not listen even now. He had smiled gently when she pointed out that Bruno had taken over some of his own clients, some of the most lucrative, at that.

'At my suggestion, my dear girl!' he had insisted. 'I'm trying to shed some of my workload. You told me I was working too hard, remember!'

'I didn't tell you to hand some of your best clients over to Bruno Falcucci! And you never told me that was what you were planning!'

He had given her a wry, apologetic look. 'I knew you'd get agitated and lecture me on your favourite subject!'

Eyes startled, she'd asked, 'What do you mean?'

'Bruno,' Charles had said, laughing softly as she flushed dark red. 'Now, don't deny it—you're paranoid where he's concerned. You think he has horns and a forked tail!'

'Yes,' she had said then, soberly. 'I don't trust him, and I only hope you aren't making a serious mistake, letting him get into such a position of power at the bank.'

Her uneasiness had not lifted a few weeks after this discussion with Charles, on the cool autumn morning when Annie sat on her desk and would not stop talking about Bruno Falcucci.

'Shoo,' she told Annie, pushing her off her desk, and Annie turned a laughing face to her.

'Oh, come on, I bet you're secretly crazy about Bruno too—you just won't admit it!'

'I'd rather date Dracula!' Martine snapped just as her office door opened.

She and Annie both looked round, both froze in confusion. Bruno stood in the doorway, his dark eyes hooded and unreadable, his powerful body briefly at rest, which she already knew was rare for him since he was perpetually in motion, a man with burning energy always racing against the clock, or himself, or the world, she wasn't sure which.

'What's Dracula got that I haven't?' he drawled, and Annie began to giggle, half in relief because he didn't seem angry, half with embarrassment because she didn't know how much of the earlier conversation he had overheard.

'Don't tempt me,' Martine said, and Bruno looked into her eyes, his mouth twisting.

'Could I?'

Annie's eyes grew enormous, fascinated. She looked from one to the other and waited to hear more.

'No,' Martine said through her teeth.

Bruno held the door open. 'Weren't you just going, Annie?' he asked in a bland voice. She hesitated, wanting to stay and eavesdrop, but Bruno's eyes were hypnotic. Reluctantly she swayed her way across the room towards him. Martine watched Bruno watch Annie. There was a distinct gleam in the dark eyes. Annie was a pocket-sized blonde Venus—high breasts, tiny waist, rounded hips—and she knew how to move to make men stare. Bruno was staring now.

Annie paused to smile up at him; Martine couldn't see her face but she saw the way Bruno smiled down at her.

'Dracula hasn't got anything you haven't got,' Annie said, and giggled.

'Then why aren't you scared?' Bruno asked and bent towards her, lip curling to show his teeth, pretending to be about to sink his fangs into her throat.

Annie shrieked in delight and fled.

Bruno straightened and looked across the room. Martine coldly met his laughing gaze and the laughter stopped; his face tightened and turned cold. He walked towards her, letting the door slam behind him.

Her nerve-ends quivered in alarm at something in his stare. He stopped beside her desk, and for an instant of panic she was afraid he was going to touch her, kiss her.

She went crimson, then white, shrinking back from him.

He watched her inexorably.

'One of these days I'm going to tell you why you can't stand the sight of me,' he said softly. 'And then you'll really hate me.'

'I already do!'

It came out before she could stop it, and she bit her lip in shock. She hadn't meant to be so up-front about her real feelings; she was horrified that she should have lost control like that. In her work she often came up against men she loathed and despised, but she knew better than to let her view of them show!

'I'm sorry,' she said edgily, not quite meeting his gaze. 'I lost my temper, please forget I said that.'

If he told Charles she knew the reaction she would get. Charles would be appalled. He was aware she didn't trust his cousin but he expected her to have a little self-control and to keep her private opinions to herself. And, in fact, so did she. She was angry with herself for losing her cool.

'I never forget anything,' Bruno murmured, and she believed him. She had already discovered what a fantastic memory he had; he seemed to know everything about every public company and many in private hands. The tiniest detail was retained in his mind and could be conjured up out of nowhere when he needed it. They used state-of-the-art computers to do work Bruno could do in his head and seemed to find child's play.

'That's up to you,' she said, trying to hide her faint dismay. No doubt one day she would pay for having lost her temper. She suspected him to be a man who took his revenge for past wounds. That was why it worried her that Charles seemed to trust him so implicitly. She was afraid that one day Bruno Falcucci would make Charles pay for the way the Redmond family had treated Bruno's mother.

She swallowed, looked at the screen in front of her and changed the subject. 'Have you seen the latest Japanese figures?'

'More or less as I predicted,' he shrugged.

'Yes, right again, as usual!' Martine said with saccharine sweetness.

He laughed. She couldn't even make him angry. It was infuriating. She wished he would go away, he was ruining her morning.

'I am rather busy,' she told him coldly. 'So unless you wanted to tell me something important...?'

'Charles just rang me from his home,' he said. 'About the Rome conference...'

'Yes?' She was flying to Rome with Charles the following day for an international banking conference, and was rather looking forward to the trip. It was ages since she had been anywhere interesting, and it would mean getting away from the office and Bruno Falcucci for a little while.

'His doctor has advised him to stay in bed for a week, so he won't be able to go,' Bruno coolly said.

'What's wrong? Is he ill?' Martine anxiously asked but Bruno shook his head.

'Just tired, I gather. A touch of flu, too, maybe. Nothing serious, but his doctor thinks he needs complete rest. He asked me to explain to you, and say how sorry he is to miss the Rome trip.'

'Of course; I understand, though,' Martine said, deeply disappointed, her face falling. 'I can't say I'm surprised, he has looked quite exhausted the last few days. He really needs a long holiday, but a week in bed would be a good start. Well, I'd better cancel everything, but I don't think we'll be able to reclaim the price of the air tickets. The hotel can be cancelled without a problem, of course.'

She put out a hand to the phone but Bruno caught hold of her wrist, his fingers cool and light, yet making her aware of their potential strength.

'No, don't cancel anything. The trip is still on, it's just that I'll be taking Charles's place.'

Martine stiffened. 'You?'

His mouth curled. 'Sorry, I know I'm no substitute for Charles in your eyes, but you'll have to put up with my company for a few days, I'm afraid. Charles wants the bank represented. He was making a speech on the pros and cons of monetarist policy and he wants me to read it to the conference.'

Martine knew all about that speech; Charles had discussed it with her at great length. She could have delivered that speech for him, if he'd asked her, but Charles hadn't even considered that, she realised, her mouth taut.

Bruno considered her expression, his brows crooked. 'Charles has a rather old-fashioned view of women's place in banking, doesn't he?'

'Which you share?' she bitterly suggested.

'You do enjoy thinking the worst of me, don't you? No, as it happens, I don't, but Charles was obviously ill and I couldn't very well argue with him. Have you got all his documentation, by the way? Tickets, etcetera?'

She nodded and began to get up. Bruno moved back just enough to let her pass; she picked up the scent of his aftershave and decided she didn't like it.

She found the folder containing all the travel documents for Charles, and handed it to Bruno.

'The name on the tickets will have to be changed. I'll do that.'

'Don't worry, my secretary will deal with it,' he said, turning to walk out. 'See you tomorrow, on the plane.'

She glared after him, half inclined not to turn up. Only her loyalty to Charles made her decide to go. Someone had to keep an eye on Bruno Falcucci.

They met at Heathrow, in fact, in a chaotic, overcrowded terminal building. All planes were delayed by fog in the London area. Bruno and Martine bought piles of newspapers and magazines, drank lots of bitter black coffee, tried to ignore screaming babies, restless children, the whine of the Tannoy, the discomfort of the seats they sat on.

At last the fog lifted and planes began to take off. They were two hours late in leaving for Rome, in the end.

The chauffeur-driven car they had ordered was not waiting to meet them when they arrived. They had to take a taxi, there were long queues and a black, relentless rain was falling. Rome sulked under sagging clouds and grey skies. Looking up, Martine felt very depressed.

By the time they got to their hotel, which sat near the top of the Spanish Steps, she was barely able to stand, and very fed up. She collected her key and went straight to her room, which turned out to be charming: beautifully furnished and with a magnificent view over the huddled roofs, towers and cupolas of the city.

The rain was still teeming down, lashing along streets, trickling down windows, spilling from the gargoyles on churches, splashing in gutters, forming rivers down the Spanish Steps.

Martine leaned on the window for a while, gazing out. There was a magnificent desolation about the scene spread out below her, and her eyes wandered from building to building, absorbing the atmosphere. Even in the rain Rome was noisy, bustling, over-full of people and vehicles. She heard the blare of horns, police whistles, people shouting to each other, people quarrelling loudly, the clatter of feet on old pavements.

Sitting there with the window open made her shiver after a while. She stood up, closed the window and went into her modern bathroom to take a long, warm, fragrant bath, pouring deliciously scented bath oils into the water before she climbed gratefully into it.

Bruno had suggested that they meet for dinner at eight o'clock in the bar. The first gathering of the conference was at nine o'clock the following day, and was scheduled to take place at another hotel, the Excelsior, which was a popular conference centre with efficient modern facilities, next door to the United States embassy and close to the via Veneto. Most of the delegates were also staying at the Excelsior, but Charles had wanted to have a peaceful bolthole to make for when conference politics grew too hectic. It often helped to be able to escape for a while. The lobbying began at breakfast and went on until well into the night, and if you could get away you had a better chance of preserving your sanity, Charles said.

After her bath, Martine went to sleep on her bed, wrapped in her thick white bathrobe, a quilt over her. Her dreams were as chaotic as the traffic in the Rome streets; she twisted and sighed in her sleep, her body restless, overheated.

She woke up with a start when someone knocked sharply on the door. For a second she was totally disorientated. While she had slept, night had fallen; the room was dark, only the flash of a neon light somewhere nearby in the city to show her the furniture, the high oblong of the window.

She lay on the bed, staring blankly; then somebody knocked on the door again, louder, peremptorily.

Stumbling off the bed, she went to the door and opened it on the chain, blinking in the light from the corridor.

It was Bruno, in evening dress, looking the way he had the night she first saw him—ultra-civilised, menacingly primitive. It was a very disturbing mix, added to which, just the sight of his smooth-skinned, closely shaven face and sleek black hair, his gleaming jet eyes, his powerful body, sent a strange quiver of weakness through her. Ever since she had met him she had been both alarmed by and hostile to him, working on instincts buried inside her, too deep for her to be quite sure what it was about the man that set all her alarm bells jangling.

'Aren't you dressed yet? We said eight o'clock,' Bruno reminded her, his gleaming eyes roaming slowly over her dishevelled, damp coils of auburn hair, her flushed face, the short white robe which left her long legs bare and revealed the deep cleft between her breasts.

She instinctively put up a hand to pull her robe lapels together to hide her breasts, and saw Bruno's mouth twist in wry comprehension.

'I must have fallen asleep,' she stammered. 'Why don't you get yourself a drink in the bar, and I'll only be ten minutes, I promise!'

She shut the door quickly, afraid he would notice she was trembling. Switching on the light, she leaned on the elaborately carved oak bed for a moment, to steady her nerves. What on earth was wrong with her? Maybe she had picked up some bug? The same one Charles had got? She wouldn't be surprised. That was how she felt—ill, feverish, weak-legged, shivery.

She didn't want to get dressed, do her hair, have dinner alone with Bruno Falcucci; she didn't feel strong enough.

But how could she get out of it? They were here representing the bank, standing in for Charles; she couldn't simply duck out of her responsibilities, she would be letting Charles down. She must pull herself together.

Her hands cold and shaking, she began to get ready. She had picked out her dress before she had her bath: a dark green velvet, figure-hugging, with a deep scoop neckline along which ran a Greek key pattern in gold thread, a tight waist and very short skirt which left her long legs bare. It was formal and elegant, but once she had put it on Martine had second thoughts.

She stared at herself in the mirror, biting her lip. She had forgotten just how tight the dress was, and how short the skirt! It made her feel half-naked. Charles had always liked the dress, that was why she had packed it, but wearing it for Charles was one thing—wearing it when she was going to spend an evening alone with Bruno Falcucci was something else. The very thought of it made her hair stand up on the back of her neck.

She looked at her watch, and groaned. There was no time to change, either. If only she hadn't fallen asleep on the bed! She still had to do her hair and her face. She picked up her brush and began to work hurriedly.

When she walked into the hotel bar she saw Bruno watching her from a table on the other side of the room and an atavistic shudder ran through her.

Déjà vu, she told herself hurriedly. That was what it was, *déjà vu*, because this was almost a re-run of the night they'd met—and she remembered with another shudder the way their reflections had shimmered in the dark glass behind the bar. It had seemed significant then; more so now.

He's dangerous to me, she thought. Dangerous to Charles. To the bank.

Yet there was something darker involved, something she had never quite faced.

She did so now. I'm afraid of him, she admitted, ice trickling down her spine. He terrifies me.

She thought of Charles's pale face and tired eyes, the sadness in his heart, and she hated Bruno Falcucci. Charles was helpless against him; he didn't have the drive or the desire to fight back if he was attacked, but Bruno wasn't going to destroy Charles if she could stop him, so she pushed her fear away and began to walk towards him through the crowded bar.

Her auburn hair glowed like dark flame in the light of chandeliers, her oval face a classical cameo, green-shadowed eyes, elegant nose, wide, full, generous red mouth. Her slender, rounded figure swayed under the tight dark green velvet, the low neckline drawing eyes to her high, white breasts, her pale legs moving gracefully, the skirt constantly sliding up to give glimpses of her slim thighs.

The lively hum of voices, the clink of glasses, the laughter, died away and people's heads turned to watch her, although Martine herself was completely unaware of her effect on the others in the bar because she was too absorbed in staying cool, getting herself under control.

The only watching eyes of which she was aware were Bruno's; she didn't meet them but she felt them fixed on her, black, brilliant, intent, and the way they watched her made a pulse beat hard in her throat.

He stood up to greet her, she slid into the deep-upholstered seat beside him, and the noise in the bar broke out again.

'That was quite an entrance!' Bruno drily said. 'What will you have to drink?'

She looked at his glass and wasn't surprised to see that it was mineral water with a twist of lime in it. 'The same as you, thanks.'

He ordered the drink and handed her a menu. 'I've already decided what I want, but take your time to choose. The food is terrific here, and as it is a special occasion I thought we might try a glass or two of an excellent Italian wine they have on their list. You do drink wine, don't you?'

'Sometimes, not often,' she agreed, looking at the menu and realising suddenly that she was hungry. She hadn't eaten on the plane because she hated unreal food, and with surprise it dawned on her that her last meal had been breakfast at the airport. 'What a huge menu! I don't know what half these dishes are!' Remembering suddenly that he was a Swiss of Italian extraction, she asked him, 'Can you recommend something?'

He shifted along the seat and leaned over her shoulder. She felt his thigh touching hers, his arm against her, smelt his cologne.

'This is probably good at this time of year,' he suggested, pointing. 'Autumn is the best time for wild mushrooms, and I love them served with seafood.'

Martine read the name of the dish falteringly: *funghi e frutti di mare.*

'Mushrooms and seafood?' she asked.

'Exactly.' Bruno's deep voice had a husky tone, she felt his warm breathing on her bare shoulder.

'OK, I'll have that,' she hurriedly said, nervously aware of his body somehow even closer. 'And I suppose I'll just have pasta for the main course.' She would have moved away then but Bruno shook his head, pointing to the menu again.

'Don't be so predictable!' he softly said, very close to her ear. 'Try the *saltimbocco* ...'

'What's that?'

'It means...hmm..."jump in the mouth"...it's veal escalope, rolled in ham, flavoured with sage, fried and then simmered in Marsala wine. Very rich, but it's a Roman speciality, you must try it once, at least. While you're in Italy, and especially in Rome, you must be more adventurous, take a few risks for once in your life!'

She tensed, picking up the undertone, the hidden meaning, and hedged instinctively. 'Risks and banking don't go together!'

'Oh, but they do,' he drawled. 'Lending money is always a risk, but if you don't gamble you don't accumulate, as you know very well. You've been working for Charles for too long. Charles has the excuse of being middle-aged, but you're not.'

'Charles isn't middle-aged!' she threw back, flushed and angry now. 'He's only in his forties.'

Bruno laughed coldly. 'That *is* middle-aged!'

'Yes, well, Charles is still very...' She broke off the sentence, not sure how she had been meaning to finish it, and Bruno finished it for her in a hard, sardonic voice.

'Attractive? Was that what you were going to say? I know you worship the ground he walks on, and I'd be curious to know why you're so fixated on a man who was at university before you were even born! Does he remind you of your father? Or didn't you have a father? If I had a crude mind, I'd suspect it might be Charles's money you were really interested in, and that thought did occur to me before I got to know you, but I've realised you aren't that materialistic. No, it's Charles himself, isn't it?' His dark eyes watched her tense profile closely. 'You have a real problem, Martine. The gap's too wide. You'd regret it bitterly sooner or later if Charles was crazy enough to take what you're dying to give him.'

Her face was burning and a choking rage filled her throat. She turned on him furiously, her green eyes stormy with resentment.

'How dare you...?' She stopped as the waiter approached. Quivering, dark red, Martine had to swallow the words boiling to get out.

Bruno was as cool as the ice-cubes in their drinks. He smiled blandly at the waiter. 'Ah, ready to take our order? Right.' He ordered for them both, without consulting Martine again, which at any other time would have infuriated her, but which she accepted without comment then because she knew she couldn't have said a word without her voice shaking.

By the time the waiter had gone Martine had had time to work out what she really wanted to say to Bruno, but, before she could start, someone else came up to their table.

Before she actually spoke, Martine picked up the heady, musky fragrance of her perfume. It enveloped them like a cloud.

'Bruno, *caro*!' a warm voice said, and Bruno got up, smiling. Martine watched coldly as he was engulfed in what looked like a very passionate embrace. The woman was in her thirties, her black hair wreathed at the back of her head in coils and pinned there with a huge black lace bow, her skin olive, but glowing with a golden tan she had not got in Italy at that time of year. She had a figure like a fairground switchback, curving in and out exaggeratedly: full, warm breasts, a tightly belted waist, with rounded hips giving a curved line to the black satin evening suit she wore. It glittered with diamanté on the neck and cuffs and hem. Diamonds shone in her ears, at her throat, at her wrists; her hands sparkled with rings, too.

She was certainly not a wallpaper person, thought Martine drily. In fact, she obviously dressed to be noticed, in every sense of the word.

The way she was kissing Bruno, they must surely have been lovers at one time. Good friends didn't kiss on the mouth like that. So, that was the sort of woman he liked?

Martine's green eyes chilled. Every little detail about him was important, told her new facts about him, might help her defeat whatever he had planned against Charles. But she wouldn't have expected him to like a woman who looked like that.

A second later, Bruno turned her way to introduce her. 'Angelina, this is a colleague from London, Martine Archer. Martine, this is the wife of an old friend of mine, Angelina Fabri.'

Martine smiled politely and coldly, offered her hand. The other woman took it, her own smile equally cool, studying her with shrewd, sophisticated eyes.

'You are in banking?' She spoke English with a strong Italian accent, her phrasing slightly off most of the time. 'Yes, I can tell you are. A career woman, obviously. And if it gives you all you need, why not? For some women it is the answer; we don't need to get married these days, after all!'

Martine kept her face cool, her teeth together, but she knew she had just been patronised and insulted.

Bruno smoothly intervened, openly amused by the instant hostility between the two women.

'I think your friends are about to leave, Angelina.'

She turned to look across the room at a group near the door, and waved, nodding.

'Yes, I must go, *caro*! Will we see you while you're here? Now, promise we will!'

'I'll do my best. Give Carlo my best wishes, tell him I'll ring, as soon as I can. Unfortunately, I have too many engagements during the conference, but my last day here is free, maybe we could meet then?'

'You must come to dinner, *caro*. Arrange it with Carlo. *Ciao*!' Angelina gave him another hug, nodded dismissively to Martine, and walked away.

Bruno sat down again, gave Martine an amused glance. 'Well, you and Angelina didn't hit it off, did you? A pity, she's a warm-hearted woman...'

'So I noticed,' Martine said.

'Miaow!' he murmured, laughing silently. 'Well, that's Angelina; it doesn't mean anything, she's always very over the top whatever she does.'

'Does her husband know she's so...fond...of you?'

The icy sting in her voice didn't bother him; his eyes had a mocking gleam in them.

'Carlo? He adores her just the way she is...they have a very happy marriage. She's a wonderful mother, they have four boys and two girls, she runs their home to perfection—Carlo's a very lucky guy and he knows it.'

Martine stared at him, uncertain now about his relationship with the Italian woman, wishing she knew the truth about that, about every other aspect of his life. What sort of man was Bruno Falcucci?

They went into dinner a few minutes later. The meal was superb; the wine matched it. Martine only intended to drink one glass, but without noticing it drank far more because the waiter kept refilling her glass.

They talked about the conference over the table at first, then as the evening wore on Martine talked less and less. She was feeling light-headed, dreamy, a heat and excitement running through her veins. Across the table Bruno watched her with those hypnotic eyes while they drank their coffee.

'Liqueur?' he suggested as the wine waiter arrived with his rattling trolley of bottles.

She hastily shook her head. 'I've already drunk too much wine. I don't want a headache in the morning.' She looked at her watch. 'In fact, I think I should be on my way to bed now; we have to get up very early, and there's a very crowded day ahead of us.'

On their way to the lift she paused to look out through the main doors at the Rome night.

'It's stopped raining. What I wanted to do this afternoon was take a walk around the city, but I couldn't go out in all that rain.'

'Why not take a short stroll now?' suggested Bruno.

'It's much too late, and I haven't got my coat with me,' she said, but she was drawn towards the door, tempted in spite of common sense.

'We needn't walk far, just look down the Spanish Steps,' Bruno said, putting an arm around her, pushing the door open.

While she was still thinking about it she found herself outside the hotel, in the warm autumn night. The torrential rain had washed the sky and the city clean; the air was soft and still, stars shone over the Roman rooftops and a crescent moon sailed above them.

'It's magical,' she breathed, staring around her. With the rain over, everyone had come out to enjoy the city. The night was full of people, walking, talking, the lights of cafés and bars, the sound of guitars, of someone singing Italian with a throb in his throat.

'You don't want to catch a chill. Put my jacket round your shoulders,' Bruno said, and she looked round in surprise as she dropped his evening jacket around her.

'What about you?' she asked. He looked like a toreador in his black trousers and waistcoat; he had that atmosphere of arrogance, high courage, disdain. 'Aren't you cold just in your shirt-sleeves and that thin waistcoat?'

He shook his head. 'Don't worry about me, I'm tough. Do you want to window-shop? If we go down the steps we'll be in the via Condotti and you can pick from Gucci, Bulgari and a lot of other designer-label places.'

'Going down the steps would be fine,' she said wryly. 'It's coming up again in this dress that could be a problem. The skirt's so tight.'

Bruno's dark eyes wandered slowly over her, lingered on her long, smooth legs. 'That dress is dynamite,' he murmured, and her colour deepened.

She turned away hurriedly and began to wander along the road. She didn't know quite how it had happened but in her dreamy mood her hostility had got lost somewhere, Charles pushed to the back of her mind. She was too wrapped up in the romance of the Rome night.

Passing a dark shop doorway, she heard a movement, a sound; there was a couple standing in the shadows, a skinny boy in jeans and a young girl in a brief tight skirt and red sweater. They were passionately kissing, bodies pressed so fiercely against each other that it was hard to say where one began and the other ended. As Martine paused to stare, the boy's hand began to slide up inside the girl's tiny skirt and the girl gave a little moan.

Martine spun to walk away and cannoned into Bruno.

He had seen the young couple too. He looked down at Martine, who was breathing raggedly, shivering as if she was cold.

'I . . . we . . . we'd better go back inside,' she stammered, her face darkly flushed.

Bruno followed her as she headed back towards the hotel, but as they passed another shop he suddenly grabbed her and pulled her into the doorway.

She gave a cry of protest, looking up angrily, and then his mouth was on her own, hard, hot, compelling. It was as if he had lit a forgotten fuse inside her; she began to shake, a flame leaping through her veins, her whole body going up in fire, an explosion that left her helpless.

Her lips parted moistly under the invasion of his tongue; she felt her legs give under her, and put her arms around his neck and clung to him, shuddering in a reaction she couldn't stop or understand.

It was a long time since anyone had made love to her. She had buried desires, needs, hungers that she refused to feel. They had betrayed her once; she wouldn't give them another chance.

Tonight though, the wine must have loosened her inhibitions, allowed her hidden emotions to escape. Deep inside her she felt the beat of an erotic drum. Her fingers clenched in his hair, closed on the firm nape of his neck, moved down his back, passionately aware of the male strength of the warm body under the evening shirt, aching to touch him more intimately, unconsciously moving invitingly against him, her hips pressing closer.

Bruno gave a thick groan, his leg sliding between her thighs, his hand under the jacket still hanging from her shoulders. She felt him unzip the velvet dress; it parted; Bruno's hand slid inside and caressed her bare back, followed the curve of her spine downwards to her buttocks, his fingers inserting themselves into the top of her tiny silk briefs.

The dark, breathing absorption they shared was suddenly broken by the sound of running feet, screams, shouting.

They spun apart, very flushed, out of breath. A teenage boy ran past the shop doorway. They saw a woman's handbag clutched in his hand. Before Bruno and Martine could move a whole string of people ran past after the boy, screaming angrily in Italian. A police whistle sounded near by; the boy dived down the Spanish Steps. The crowd followed him.

The sound of the pursuit died away into the city. Martine shakily did up her zip without looking at Bruno, her head averted. All the excited heat had evaporated, and she was suddenly very cold.

'Come to my room, Martine,' Bruno said with an urgency that made her stiffen.

She turned on him, her face white now. 'I feel sick, do you know that?' she broke out. 'You got me drunk, you knew I wasn't used to drinking, and you kept pouring wine into me, right the way through dinner. You had this in mind all the time, didn't you? You set me up, and it nearly worked. I almost fell for the oldest trick in the book.'

There was a silence you could have cut with a knife. His eyes turned to glittering black ice. 'You did fall for it,' he drawled, admitting her accusations, mocking her. 'I could have had you if that stupid boy hadn't come past here when he did! After all those years of waiting for Charles to finally notice that you're a woman, you're so frustrated that you fell into my hands like a ripe peach, and I didn't even have to try very hard.'

She hit out at him, he ducked and she hurt her hand on the edge of the shop window. Gasping in pain, she shed his evening jacket, let it fall to the floor, and as he bent to retrieve it Martine turned and ran, holding back tears, fighting not to give way to the waves of emotion swamping her. Two minutes later she was back in the hotel, in the safety of lights and other people. She didn't know whether Bruno followed her or not. The lift was standing open and she ran into it at once, pressed the floor button, the doors closed and she was taken up to her room.

Once she was in there, behind locked doors, she could start to cry.

CHAPTER THREE

MARTINE had her breakfast in her room: black coffee, orange juice, a couple of rolls with black cherry jam. She had slept badly but a careful make-up job hid most of the evidence of that and she deliberately picked out a smoothly tailored dark grey suit, short jacket, straight skirt, with a crisp white shirt under it, to make herself fade into the crowd, mostly men, in city suits, who would be attending the conference. Even her auburn hair was pulled back austerely from her face, but she could do little about her long legs in their sheer black stockings. Men always stared at them.

A car was coming at eight-twenty to take Bruno and herself to the Excelsior Hotel for the opening meeting of the conference. Martine left her room at eight-fifteen, and arrived down in the foyer exactly as the chauffeur-driven car arrived. Bruno appeared a moment later, elegant and formal in a dark city suit, red and white striped shirt with a stiff white collar and a sombre wine-red silk tie. Over the suit he wore a black cashmere overcoat, unbuttoned, thrown open.

She gave him a cool nod. 'Good morning,' she said for the benefit of the waiting driver.

Bruno's eyes were frozen wastes, and he answered her in a tone equally distant. 'Good morning.'

They drove side by side in the back of the car, each looking out into the crowded, noisy streets, neither speaking.

It was a short drive; the city lay around them like a living, breathing being. Everywhere they went Martine saw broken stone arches, columns of marble, great pillared churches; heard a continual sound of bells from steeples around the city, the clatter of pigeons in a square they drove through. She watched the birds rise up, wings iridescent against the blue of an autumn morning, heard the splash of fountains, some of them inhabited by magnificent statues, Neptune with a trident, cherubs, dolphins; and everywhere Martine saw flocks of priests in black and nuns with rosary beads rattling as they hurried along.

People said all cities looked alike these days— they couldn't include Rome. It was unlike any city Martine had ever seen.

She stared out at it from the car, feeling as if her every nerve-end had been intensely sensitised; each brief sensation she experienced was sending ripples of response throughout her nervous system.

Bruno leaned back in the corner beside her, his body swaying with the movement of the car. She fought not to look at him, but couldn't stop her eyes wandering sideways once, glimpsing his dark-clad, muscled thigh; one leg crossed over the other, his arm resting on his knee, his hand splayed, long, powerful fingers at ease.

Heat rose in her throat; she was remembering last night, that hand sliding intimately down inside her dress.

Swallowing, she looked away, her skin burning. The mere memory was enough to make her stomach churn. How could she have let him do that to her? Have wanted it? Because she had; she had been going crazy while he touched her, she couldn't deny it.

It was the wine, she told herself hurriedly. That was what had made her crazy: the wine. She wasn't used to drinking, and she certainly wasn't going to touch the stuff again.

It was a relief to reach the hotel. They had to go through Security first, hand over their identification and documents; be given an electronic pass with their name and country of origin, and the name of their bank, digitally recorded on tape on the surface.

'You must wear your pass at all times during the sessions,' they were informed. 'Or you will not be permitted into the conference hall.'

The proceedings began promptly at nine. There were hundreds of delegates seated in rows for this inaugural session, long addresses by very important people in international finance, from the dais; but after the coffee-break at half-past ten many people left for discussions in smaller groups in smaller rooms.

Martine stayed with the general session; Bruno left to take part in one of the groups who were discussing interest rates and the consequences of manipulating them. Martine listened to a series of speeches on market forces, third-world borrowing and debts, the dangers of over-lending.

Lunch was a buffet affair. You lined up to choose from an enormous range of cold or hot food and sat wherever you could find a place.

Carrying her plate of very attractively dressed salad towards a table which still had some empty seats, Martine found herself sitting next to someone she knew—Gerhard von Essenberg, an attractive man in his early thirties, an observer at the conference for the German Bundesbank.

'Lovely to see you, darling,' he said as he kissed her. His tones were those of someone who had spent a couple of years in the sixth form at Charterhouse, the English public school which turned out more city men than any other, before going to university in Germany and then on to MIT in the States for a year before taking up a career in banking. 'Is Charles here too?'

'No, he was to have been, but he has flu,' Martine told him.

'Oh, too bad. Poor Charles.'

They had met in London a year earlier at a reception at the German embassy in Belgrave Square. While he was in London Gerhard had dated Martine twice; they had seen a play together and gone ice-skating, at which Martine was hopeless but at which Gerhard was quite brilliant. He had skated as a child, on frozen lakes and rivers near his home in Germany, he said; she really should visit him there one day.

Charles knew all about him; he said he was a very rich young man from an old German family. Gerhard was fair, faintly cold, very clever. Theirs had been a brief relationship, they'd only known each other for a week; it had been an interlude; hardly a friendship, let alone a romance. But she was pleased to see him.

'We must try to sit together over dinner,' he said.

'We've been allocated seats,' she pointed out, but Gerhard shrugged.

'Oh, I'm sure we can change our seats if we ask. I'm bored by the people I'm with—frightful fellows who talk of nothing but money. Who are you sitting with? Do you know?'

She had been seated next to Bruno. 'A colleague,' she said offhandedly. 'I'd rather sit with you, if it's possible.'

'Anything is possible,' Gerhard said with the faint arrogance of his upbringing and class, and smiled at her with a charm that was entirely his own. 'Now, tell me all your news! Is there a man in your life?'

She shook her head. 'Not at the moment. Have you met the girl of your dreams yet?'

He laughed. 'I keep hoping, but so far no luck.'

'Maybe you're too difficult to please!'

'I've been brought up to expect the best,' he agreed with wry amusement. 'No doubt you're right, but never mind, I enjoy my life. I'm free, single and love to mingle, as they say on TV.'

She laughed. 'You still watch Sky MTV all the time?'

'All the time. When I work at home, I have the TV on with the music programme blaring out—it helps me think, keeps me awake during long night sessions.'

'I wonder how people managed before recorded music!' Martine said thoughtfully.

'My family had their own personal chamber orchestra in the eighteenth century,' Gerhard said casually.

'Good heavens!' Martine said, stunned.

'My father still loves that sort of music; he listens to Mozart, I listen to Guns 'n' Roses. The difference is, I like his music, too; but he hates mine.'

Martine ate her salad slowly, listening to him. She was just finishing her coffee when the delegates began to drift away; the conference was starting again in fifteen minutes. She looked at her watch and sighed.

'Time to get back. See you later.'

She got up and Gerhard rose, too. He bent and kissed her lightly on the mouth. 'Meet me for drinks before dinner in the bar, OK? Seven o'clock?'

She nodded. 'Seven. OK.'

As she turned to go she saw Bruno, at the next table, watching her with the cold eyes of an enemy.

Martine felt a leap of shock, the blood left her face. Pulling herself together, she walked away fast.

They were both in the main hall that afternoon, seated next to each other because the seats had been numbered in advance and one had to sit in the seat one was allocated. Martine tried to concentrate on the meeting, to ignore the fact that Bruno was so close, but she couldn't shut out her awareness of him.

Every time he shifted on his chair, every time he turned a page in his conference programme, every time he moved his head, Martine was deeply conscious of it. She even found herself listening to his breathing at one time, and was angry with herself.

Why was this happening to her? She had been working with him for months in London. She disliked, distrusted, suspected Bruno Falcucci—so why should she suddenly have become so intensely aware of him that she found it hard to think of anything else?

She was relieved when the business of the day finally ended and everyone began to filter towards the door to go back to their rooms.

'Our car will be waiting,' Bruno said offhandedly, and she nodded, following him towards the foyer. The porter went outside to whistle up their waiting vehicle, parked nearby, and Martine climbed into the back of it.

Bruno talked casually about the last discussion they had heard; Martine wondered when to tell him that she would be sitting with Gerhard for dinner.

When they reached their own hotel they took the lift upstairs. They were on the same floor, their rooms adjoining. As they approached the door of her room, Martine blurted out, 'By the way, I've been asked to join a friend for dinner tonight.'

Bruno halted outside her door, his face stiffening. 'The "friend" I saw you having lunch with?'

'Yes,' she said, defiance in her green eyes.

'You make friends quickly,' he said with cold derision.

'I've known Gerhard for ages,' she retorted. 'Charles introduced him to me last year, in London.'

Bruno's smile was sarcastic. 'Oh, well, if he's a friend of Charles's you must be nice to him, of course!'

She resented the emphasis. 'Charles would certainly expect me to be friendly to him. Gerhard is with the Bundesbank.'

'Would he expect you to sleep with him too?'

The words cut like a knife and Martine went red then white, so taken aback that for a minute she was simply dumb. She got out her key and turned to unlock her door, but Bruno hadn't finished yet.

'Because judging by the way he kept looking you over,' he threw at her back, 'that was what was on his mind as an after-dinner entertainment. From where I sat I could see him practically undressing you with his eyes.'

'You've got a one-track mind!' she angrily muttered, trying to get her key into the lock with trembling hands.

'It's a track most men follow, especially with someone who looks like you!'

At last she managed to turn the stiff key, pushed the door open, could finally escape from him. 'All men aren't like you, thank heavens!' she said over her shoulder.

'Well, don't say I didn't warn you,' Bruno grated.

He turned on his heel and walked away to his own room; she slammed her door, trembling with rage and agitation.

She had a long bath to unwind, determined to get herself into a mood to enjoy the evening. She had only brought two cocktail dresses, and one long evening dress for the formal ball which would wind up the conference. This evening she had intended to wear the dress she had worn the previous evening, since she would have to wear one short dress twice, but somehow she couldn't face putting the dark green velvet on again.

Every time she wore it in future she would be reminded of those moments in the dark shop doorway, of Bruno's mouth and hands, of the wild desire he had awakened in her.

She took out of the wardrobe a filmy black chiffon with a skirt that floated around her legs as she walked. Through the chiffon her throat and breasts took on a glimmering pallor; her dark auburn hair glowed with the colour of leaves in the autumn. She clasped a necklace of pearls round her throat, brushed glittery green shadow along her lids, painted her mouth a deep russet red, stood back from the mirror and contemplated her reflection uncertainly.

The dress was as sophisticated as the green velvet, but somehow... She broke off, frowning, biting her lip. Somehow sexier, she uneasily admitted. All that skin showing through the black gauzy material... maybe she should wear the green velvet?

No, she couldn't bear to. She turned away. She had to leave or she would be late. She didn't wait for Bruno; she took a taxi back to the conference hotel and found Gerhard waiting in the bar when she walked in, dead on seven.

His blue eyes skated over her as she walked towards him, and she remembered Bruno's accusation. He practically undresses you with his eyes, Bruno had said, and Gerhard was certainly staring, but Martine didn't find the way he looked at her offensive.

He stood up, kissed her on both cheeks gravely. 'Thank you for joining me. All the men are going to envy me tonight, having you for a partner. That dress is very sexy, and you look breathtaking in it.'

'Thank you, Gerhard,' she said, sitting down, brushing down her filmy skirts as they hissed silkily around her legs.

'What will you have to drink?' he asked, summoning a waiter.

Remembering what had happened with Bruno the previous evening, Martine ordered a mixture of orange juice and mineral water, and stayed off wine all evening.

The meal was superb, Gerhard kept her continuously amused and it would have been a wonderful evening if she hadn't been able to see Bruno from where she was sitting. By bad luck, however, he was seated facing her, on the next table; she had to avoid letting her eyes wander that way or she found herself all too often looking straight at him.

Every time it happened she felt a strange, dizzying lurch, as if her sense of balance had just gone and at any minute she might fall over.

It was disconcerting and disturbing. She became more and more afraid of the sensation. You would expect it to lessen after a while, as she kept seeing Bruno, but it didn't. On the contrary it was getting worse, the effect lasting longer. She would catch sight of him and feel the clutch of vertigo, her pulses hammering, her mouth dry, her head spinning. Hurriedly she would look away but the strange sensations went on and on, making it almost impossible to keep up a polite pretence of interest in what Gerhard was saying. She kept feeling she needed to hold on to something solid—the table, a chair, anything to give her some stability, stop this terrible whirling of the senses.

She was relieved when the meal was over and they all drifted out to the bar again. Martine let Gerhard find a table, agreed to have a crème de menthe liqueur, served on a pyramid of chipped ice; she sipped it slowly, through a straw, making it last half an hour. They had been joined by other Germans from Deutsche Bank, the biggest bank in Germany. They all knew Gerhard, who was a well-known sportsman and a leading light in the sporting activities of the Bundesbank when they played the other German banks at rugger and tennis and squash.

Martine was able to sink back into her chair and listen to them all, without needing to say a word, especially when they kept forgetting she was present and lapsed into German. She knew a little, but not enough to follow a rapid conversation, especially on international banking issues.

At eleven o'clock Bruno appeared beside their table. Martine stiffened as soon as she saw him. The Deutsche Bank people looked round, breaking into smiles and began chattering away to him in German in a way that made it clear they knew him. Martine picked up a phrase or two and realised they were asking him why he had left Switzerland to work in London. Bruno shrugged, replying in their language, and whatever he said made them all laugh.

He glanced coolly across their heads at her. 'Our car's here. Ready?'

Gerhard stirred, looking round at her. 'Darling, I can see you home in a taxi later—you don't want to leave yet, do you?'

Before she could say anything Bruno answered for her crisply. 'We all have to be up early; tomorrow is going to be a demanding day. Hurry up, Martine, we don't want to keep our driver waiting.'

She stumbled to her feet, very flushed, murmured something apologetic to Gerhard, who made a face, but bent to kiss her.

'Maybe he's right, your spoilsport friend? We have a lot to get through tomorrow. OK, sleep well, darling. I'll be seeing you at lunch, perhaps, if we are both free?'

She followed Bruno out of the hotel, got into the waiting car, secretly rather relieved to be leaving because she had been bored with all the banking talk, especially in a language she found it hard to follow, yet at the same time irritated because Bruno was ordering her about, making decisions for her, answering for her.

As they drove through the warm Rome night she muttered to him, 'Will you stop giving me orders as if I were here as your secretary? I'm Charles's private assistant, not yours. He never pushes me around, he treats me with respect, and I'd like you to do the same, please.'

'If I hadn't interrupted your little party you might have been there all night, and then you would have been in no shape to take part in the conference tomorrow,' he coldly said. 'I'm delivering Charles's speech, at eleven, remember; you ought to be there in case there are questions. I might need to consult you on what you think Charles's view might be on some issues. I'm simply his mouthpiece as far as the speech is concerned, and I may not know all the answers to the questions I'm asked, whereas I imagine you will. You make it your business to know everything there is to know about Charles and his opinions.'

'Don't use that sarcastic tone to me!' Martine broke out, her body tense, her face flushed.

'Merely stating the facts,' he drawled. 'If you don't like them it's because you prefer not to face up to the truth.'

The car pulled up outside the hotel. She climbed out, walked through the foyer, collected her key and went towards the lifts. Bruno caught up with her there; she ignored him, her head turned away.

The lift took them up to their floor, they walked to their rooms, Martine slightly ahead, Bruno strolling just behind her. She opened her door but before she could shut it Bruno's foot jammed it open. Tensing, Martine swung round to face him.

'What...?'

'We need to talk, before the conference. I suggest we have breakfast together downstairs at a quarter to eight.'

'I prefer to breakfast in my room.'

His black eyes glittered angrily. 'A quarter to eight, downstairs,' he repeated. 'Be there.'

'Get your foot out of my door!'

'Are you trying to make me lose my temper?' Bruno ground out between his teeth.

'What happens if you do?' she mocked him scornfully. Did he think he could frighten her into obeying him? 'Do you turn green like the Incredible Hulk and burst out of your clothes?'

He wasn't amused, a dark colour in his face, his voice harsh. 'Very funny.'

She had a reckless impulse, and gave in to it, her head tossed back defiantly. 'And for the record you were wrong about Gerhard—he was an angel all evening, a perfect gentleman.'

Bruno laughed without humour. 'Because I came and got you before the evening ended!' His eyes flared, a sudden hard rage in them, and he deliberately looked her up and down, from her warm red mouth to her bared shoulders, down over the filmy black chiffon through which her pale flesh glowed like pearl. 'If you'd come back here with him in a taxi late at night, looking like that, he wouldn't just have seen you to your door and said goodnight. That dress is an invitation to do more than dance, and he would have expected to be asked to stay the night.'

His insulting stare had made her turn red, hating him. 'I ought to slap your face!'

'Try it,' he said, his teeth showing in a barbed smile. 'And by the way, I asked around about Gerhard von Essenberg. He's from an old German family, and he's tipped to climb in the Bundesbank, but he doesn't have the sort of money Charles Redmond has, so even if you do fancy von Essenberg I should go on hoping Charles will finally propose, if I were you. The other guy is closer to your age, but he hasn't got as much to offer.'

It was the final straw. Martine was tired, it had been a difficult day; she lost her temper. Her hand shot up towards his face, but Bruno was too quick for her. He caught her wrist, dragged her hand down again so hard that Martine fell forward.

She found her face buried in his shirt, her nostrils filling with the scent of his body, and went into mindless panic, making muffled sounds of fear, fighting to get away. Bruno took hold of her shoulders, she struggled, there was a tearing noise, and she felt the black chiffon over her shoulders ripping, and cried out wordlessly as one side of her dress tumbled down, leaving part of her breast naked.

Along the corridor a door opened, a face peered out, perhaps disturbed by the noise she was making, and Bruno quickly pushed Martine back into her room and followed, closing the door behind them.

'Get out!' she whispered hoarsely, holding her dress up, trembling violently.

'Martine——' he began, but she couldn't take any more.

'If you don't get out of here now I'll start to scream!'

'You're over-reacting,' he began again and Martine opened her mouth to scream.

Before she could get a sound out his hand was over her lips and he was pushing her backwards, away from the door. She hadn't yet put on the light, the room was pitch-black, she couldn't see him, but she fought him wildly, like a trapped animal.

Suddenly her foot caught the leg of a chair, she stumbled backwards and fell, unable to save herself. Bruno went with her. He landed heavily on top of her, on the carpet, knocking all the breath out of her.

Martine's auburn hair had fallen down, had tumbled over her face, long, silky strands blinding her. She was gasping, shaking, fiercely aware of Bruno's weight holding her down, of the power of that male body as it lay on her.

There was a thick silence; she looked through her hair and saw his face dimly, his black eyes staring down at her, glittering in the dark room like torchlight, setting her on fire.

He made a rough sound in his throat, then his head came down and his mouth was on hers, ruthlessly forcing her lips apart and invading between them, his hands clasping her face, holding her head so that she couldn't escape the probing intimacy of the kiss. Martine struggled helplessly, briefly, half fainting and feeling he would suffocate her at any moment. Her pulses were hammering at neck and wrist and between her breasts; she closed her eyes, a little moan escaping her as she stopped fighting.

Ever since they got to Rome she had been fighting an erotic awareness of him. She didn't understand it, but she couldn't silence it, this beating sensuality whenever Bruno came near her. Every time she saw him she caught herself staring; her mouth went dry; she was hot one minute, cold the next, locked in feverish response to him.

I don't like him; why do I feel like this? I don't trust him, I don't understand him, she told herself, and then, as his mouth slid hotly down her throat, making her shudder with aroused excitement, Oh, God, but I want him.

He pushed aside the torn fragments of her bodice and she groaned as he kissed her naked breast. Her hand went up to clasp the back of his head, and she twisted restlessly underneath him.

Bruno lifted his head, breathing raggedly, his fingers splayed warmly against her body. 'If you don't want this, say so now, while I can still stop,' he whispered in a voice so husky that she only just understood what he'd said.

At the same time his hand was softly moving up her thigh, the intimate brush of his skin on hers making her quiver in hungry response.

'Say something,' he murmured, even more husky, and she kept her eyes closed, groaning.

'Sssh...'

He made a sound like breathless laughter. 'Don't say I didn't give you a chance to say no,' he said, his hand slipping underneath her.

The zip of her dress smoothly ran down, then the silky folds of material slid down her body with a gentle murmur. She shivered in her bra and panties, starting to wake up from the overheated dream, beginning to realise what she was doing. Bruno was kicking off his trousers; he sat up to take off his shirt and she felt cold as the warmth of his body was taken away. Panic surged back into her.

'No,' she said, getting up, stumbling across the room, away from him. 'I must have been out of my mind...I can't...'

She made for the light switch but Bruno caught up with her before she reached it.

'Don't run away from it now, Martine, not now we've got this far,' he whispered in a smoky voice, his arms going round her from behind, pulling her back against his half-naked body, and she shuddered as their flesh touched, skin on skin, the roughness of his hair, the masculinity of bone and muscle imposing themselves, making her deeply conscious of her own femininity.

'I should never have let you touch me,' she said, as much to herself as him, hating herself because she felt the inexorable rise of desire again.

'You're not a virgin?' he murmured, kissing her neck, pressing himself against her.

'What's that got to do with it? I don't just sleep with anyone...'

'I never supposed you did. I wouldn't want you if I thought you had,' he said, and his hands covered her breasts, making her tremble with passion.

'But why...?' she cried out, trying to think clearly, to work out what she really felt.

'Why do I want you?' He sighed, his long, naked thigh pushing softly against her, his hands wandering, exploring, making her so weak that she was shaking violently. 'You're beautiful. The minute I saw you I knew I had to have you.'

She had felt the same, she knew that at that instant. When they were jammed in that revolving door together she had felt his body against hers and a heat had begun deep inside her, a heat which had been growing ever since, and which just the sight of him could start into life.

She was torn between an aching need and fear. 'I...I haven't taken any precautions,' she muttered.

'Don't worry, I'll take care of that,' he said at once, and spun her round to face him, held her lightly by the hips, drawing her closer.

She gave a groan, stood on tiptoe and kissed him passionately, her arms going round his neck, her body yielding in boneless surrender.

Bruno lifted her off her feet and on to the bed. He didn't give her another chance to change her mind. While she was still catching her breath he entered her and she arched to take him, a wordless primitive cry coming from her throat.

For months desire had been driving her towards this instant. She had fought it, tried to pretend it wasn't happening to her, but it had been too strong, she had been helpless against it. She didn't know even now whether she was in love, or merely obsessed, she only knew she couldn't fight how she felt any more.

Last, night, when they had walked along the top of the Spanish Steps in the warm autumn night and she'd seen the young lovers in that shop doorway, that had been the moment when she'd known she wanted Bruno like that.

She had seen those two kissing, their bodies straining against each other, and suddenly she had felt heat sweep through her, her mouth had gone dry, and Bruno had looked at her with the same craving in his eyes.

She had wanted to go to bed with him then. If they had been up here, in her room, they would have made love. She had known it last night, she knew it now. If she hadn't slept with him now she would have, one day, sooner or later, because she couldn't stop thinking about it, day and night. The beat of that erotic desire drummed in her blood, in her ears; she had ached to touch him, to feel his hair under her hands, to hold his body as he moved in her, with her.

She cried out, her nails digging into his back, and Bruno groaned, head flung back in passionate pleasure.

His skin was red-hot, his breathing tortured; so was hers. She was caught up in the vortex of a whirlpool, irresistibly engulfed in a spiralling pleasure. She was deaf, dumb, blind to everything else in the world; entirely taken over by desire. She had shed all inhibitions; forgotten where they were, what room, in what city, in what country. There was only this bed, her body twisting and shuddering with his body driving into her.

She said his name, pleading, moaning. It seemed to be taking forever to reach the intense, dark heart of that feeling; she was going out of her mind, and she pushed her face into his warm, bare shoulder, kissed his perspiring skin, tasted the salt of his body on her tongue and grazed him with her teeth, bit him as the frenzy mounted, and then the aching tension broke and she gave a final long, moaning cry and began to fall down, down, out of all control.

It was like dying, her heart pounding, her lungs tortured, her limbs trembling violently.

She heard Bruno saying her name, his voice unrecognisable, gasping out in the same unbelievable ferocity; and then there was silence and she lay like someone who had drowned, her arms flung out on either side, her eyes closed, her lips apart, breathing in dragging anguish.

For minutes on end they just lay there, his body heavy on her, his head on her breast, the sweat running between them.

Then Bruno slowly slid off and lay beside her, his breathing gradually slowing. Martine was too exhausted to move. She couldn't even open her eyes.

He got up and went into her bathroom. She winced as light stabbed into the dark bedroom, put her arm across her face, and turned on to her side, her back to the light. He came back and got into bed again; by then she was half asleep and only stirred lightly as she felt his cooler flesh touch her when he curved his body round hers. He pulled a sheet over them both, but she hardly noticed. She was light as air, empty, drained. Moments later she was deeply asleep.

When she woke up in the morning he was gone.

CHAPTER FOUR

MARTINE might almost have thought she had dreamt the night before, except that as she sat up in bed she saw a note on the hotel's distinctive paper, lying on the pillow next to her, and recognised his bold and flowing handwriting.

The message was brief, almost curt. 'Breakfast 7.45 downstairs. B.' That was all it said. He didn't even say good morning. He hadn't even signed it with his name, just with an impersonal initial.

She ran a fingertip over the writing, as if she was touching him; felt her insides dissolve helplessly.

Bruno, she thought. Images of last night ran through her head and she trembled.

And then the phone rang shrilly, making her jump. She looked at it as if it was a snake and might bite. Then suddenly she thought: maybe it's him, ringing to say all the things he didn't put in that note?

A flush sprang into her face; she lifted the receiver, huskily said, 'Hello?'

'Good morning, this is your operator; it is seven-fifteen, *signorina*,' said the over-cheerful Italian voice.

'Oh... thank you...' Martine put the receiver back. She hadn't asked for a wake-up call; Bruno must have booked it.

Well, that had been thoughtful of him, and no doubt he had gone back to his own room very early, so that nobody should see him leaving hers, which was very considerate. Everyone on this floor was at the conference and some of them knew her; gossip could spread like wildfire at these events. She could remember at other conferences listening to gleeful talk of who was sleeping with whom; these things did happen when people were away from home and went in for long, long dinners with the wine flowing freely.

But her and Bruno...that was different! she thought with anguish. That hadn't just been a one-night stand at a conference, something to be forgotten about as soon as possible. Or...had it?

She sat very still on the edge of the bed, staring at that brief, cold, impersonal note. It was hardly a love-letter, was it?

He could have said something about last night, or at least signed his name. 'Love, Bruno' wouldn't have compromised him, would it?

Had last night meant anything to him, other than an easy conquest? He hadn't said he loved her; he hadn't made any promises. One minute they had been quarrelling at her door, the next they were on the floor, making love in a frenzy.

Her face burnt as she remembered those moments on the floor, on the bed; the intensity of passion they had shared.

Stricken, she screwed the note up and threw it across the room. What had she done? She'd never behaved that way before in her life, never been promiscuous, and now was a lousy time to start. She wished she could go back in time, turn back the clock, wipe out those moments in his arms.

She was twenty-seven, not inexperienced—she'd had a couple of serious relationships: one that had lasted for over a year before breaking up by mutual consent; the second the affair that had been so painful that she hadn't wanted to get involved with anybody else for a long, long time.

But no other man had made her feel the way she had last night. She hadn't even suspected that such incredible sensuality existed. It had been like flying; she had flung herself recklessly from a mountain peak and found to her astonished gratitude that she had wings, and she had been so sure he felt the same.

She shut her eyes, remembering his passion. That hadn't been faked! But maybe she had misunderstood—good sex didn't need emotion behind it. Had she forgotten that some men just liked sex, and could walk away afterwards without looking back, however good it had been?

Was Bruno like that? Oh, God, how was she going to face him this morning? The thought of breakfast made her want to throw up. Eating breakfast with him, having to look at him, remembering, knowing that he remembered.

She remembered her first impression of him. The good looks cloaked ruthless determination; he had killer's eyes, a mind like a computer. It made him good at his job, but a poor risk as a lover. That was the man who took you last night, she thought with a pang of stricken shame. As soon as he sensed that for some reason you were vulnerable to him, he took what he could, and then walked away.

How had he known he could do that? How had she betrayed herself? White, she felt her stomach heaving. A hand over her mouth, she ran into the bathroom and was violently sick.

She sat on the floor, sobbing, for minutes on end, a cold wet towel against her feverish face.

She couldn't stay there; she had to go down to breakfast, because he was capable of coming up here to get her. She didn't want him walking back into her bedroom. The very idea made her want to throw up again.

She showered and put on a dark grey pleated skirt, a lemon shirt, a grey waistcoat over that. She combed her auburn hair into an elegant French pleat and did her make-up, clipped neat silver earrings into her ears, then considered her reflection. She wanted to look businesslike, cool, remote.

Bruno Falcucci wasn't going to find any weaknesses in her today; never again, in fact.

She had lied to herself for too long; kept telling herself she hated him when she was secretly carrying a torch for him. Last night the torch had set her on fire, but it had burnt out now, all that was left was blackened earth and emptiness. Now she really did hate Bruno Falcucci. She would be armoured against him from now on.

She collected her conference briefcase, the notes, the folders, the printed material they kept being handed and never had time to read.

Head up, she took a deep breath and went down to the dining-room. She paused in the door, swallowing.

Yes. He was already there, sipping orange juice, turning the pink pages of a copy of the *Financial Times*, no doubt yesterday's paper. Today's issue would not have reached Rome yet.

This morning he looked grimly formidable in a dark suit, the jacket open to show his tight-fitting waistcoat, immaculate white shirt and dark blue silk tie. His face was closely shaven, unshadowed, his black hair sleek—he looked as if he had had a great night's sleep, damn him, unlike her. He must be as cold as ice. And last night she had been utterly convinced he wanted her as much as she wanted him.

She watched as he put his half-finished glass of juice down, his long fingers steady. Hard to believe those hands had taken her into heaven last night.

She flinched from the memory of his lovemaking; bit her lip and tasted the salt of her own blood in her mouth. Damn him. Damn him.

He closed his newspaper, glanced up, caught sight of her, his eyes narrowing, searching her face. What was he looking for? A sign of how much he had hurt her? She showed him a shuttered face; saw his brows flick together as if he was disappointed. If he thought he was having any more fun at her expense, he was mistaken, she thought grimly, walking towards him.

He rose to his feet. 'Good morning.' He came round to hold her chair for her, and she sat down, very conscious of him as he pushed her chair inwards again, unable to hide the flinch she gave as his hand brushed her shoulder.

Bruno gave her another of those piercing looks, his black eyes chilly. 'Did you sleep well?'

The bite in his tone didn't escape her. She wanted to yell, hit him, but she fought to keep her face as icy as his own.

'Yes, thank you. Did you?'

Before he could answer, the waiter arrived. She ordered coffee, orange juice, prunes with natural yoghurt, and toast.

When the waiter had gone, she asked Bruno stiffly, 'What did you want to talk about, anyway?'

'Your opinions on the conference discussions, obviously; or of what you'd heard so far,' he coolly said, as if they were mere acquaintances. 'You're making notes all the time in the conference hall, I noticed.'

He noticed everything, she thought. 'For Charles,' she said aloud.

His mouth twisted. 'Of course.' His eyes stabbed at her across the table suddenly. 'Did you make notes last night, for Charles?'

White, she whispered back, 'Shut up. Damn you. Shut up.'

The waiter came smilingly back with her orange juice and the prunes and yoghurt, poured her a large cup of fresh coffee, offered cream or hot milk.

'Black, thank you,' she said hoarsely, spooning the creamy white yoghurt over her prunes, feeling her stomach churn at the very idea of eating them, but forcing herself to do so.

She had to seem normal, calm, unworried; at all costs she mustn't let him guess how much damage he had done her.

The waiter refilled Bruno's cup. 'I'll bring your toast now.'

When he walked away, Bruno said in his remote, cool voice, 'May I read your notes, or are they only for Charles's eyes?'

Martine glanced at him secretly through her lowered lashes, hating him. 'You mean is there anything about you in them? No, there isn't, and there won't be, don't worry. I won't be telling Charles any private anecdotes.'

'I'm sure you won't,' he said, his voice stinging. 'Hasn't it occurred to you yet that I might?'

Her face grew taut, white as bone. She watched him with bitter contempt. 'Was that what it was all about? Was that your game plan? You got me into bed so you could tell Charles and wreck my...'

'Chance with him?' he drawled, mouth twisting.

'Reputation!' she said. 'I know how ambitious you are; I think you see me as some sort of threat to your plans. If I married Charles I'd stand in your way, wouldn't I? But I didn't think even you would sink to seducing me just so that you could run off and tell Charles about it!'

That got home. Dark red filled his face, and he looked at her savagely. 'And I wouldn't! I'm not the type to kiss and tell, you needn't worry.'

'Am I supposed to say thank you now?' she asked icily.

There was a barbed silence, then Bruno clipped out, 'What about your conference notes? Can I see them or not?'

'Oh, why not?' she wearily said. 'But they're in shorthand.'

'I can read shorthand.'

'I might have known you could,' Martine said bitterly. 'You're an expert at everything, aren't you?' Including seducing women. He was very good at that. He must have had a lot of practice to be that expert.

His black eyes glittered, but he answered flatly. 'I did a business course, before I went to university: shorthand, typing, computers. I've found it very useful.'

She tried to match his level tone. 'I use a rather scribbled shorthand of my own, though. Wouldn't you rather wait until the notes have been typed?'

'Not unless this is your roundabout way of refusing to let me see them.'

'Oh, very well,' she said, knowing he left her no choice, got out her notepad, and handed it to him.

'I'll read it some time today and let you have it back before we leave,' he said, putting it into his own briefcase.

The waiter arrived with their toast; Martine took one thin slice, spread it with black cherry jam, pretended to eat some. Bruno ate his with marmalade. They talked about the conference while they finished their breakfast, then Bruno looked at his watch.

'The car must be here by now, we'd better go.'

The drive to the Excelsior seemed endless, the car claustrophobic, stifling her and making her feel like screaming, shut up in it with Bruno, his body far too close, every movement he made tearing at her nerves and making her sweat.

She was so tense that as they got out of the car to go into the conference she caught her heel on the kerb. Bruno put an arm around her, to stop her falling, and as their bodies touched Martine had that familiar dizzying sense of the world spinning round her.

She pushed him away, trembling, and as she did so caught sight of a dark red graze on the side of his throat, just under his ear.

Heat enveloped her as she realised what it was. She had bitten him last night, in the last moments of their lovemaking. She hadn't realised she was leaving such obvious marks. What if someone noticed, made a joke about it? She would want to sink through the floor!

'Oh, for God's sake, stop looking at me like that!' Bruno snapped, his face icily hostile. 'You're as safe as houses with me after last night. I won't be trying my luck again. Charles is welcome to you.'

He turned on his heel and walked away and she slowly followed, fighting tears.

Bruno's delivery of Charles's speech was impressive; he had the full attention of the conference, and a number of questions were asked, all of which he was able to answer without needing to consult her.

There were a group of women from one of the big American merchant banks sitting behind Martine, who overheard their whispered comments.

'He's good, isn't he?' one of them said. 'I wonder what his view is on international intervention?'

'I wonder what he's like in bed,' one of the others said dreamily, and a little gale of laughter went up from them all.

Martine felt her face burning. She was glad nobody she knew was near enough to have overheard the conversation and notice her blush; they might have put two and two together.

The day dragged on; Gerhard was having lunch with some important members of the German banking fraternity and she only saw him briefly, in a corridor. Bruno was busy, too; at least she was spared the torture of his company that afternoon, and when their car arrived there was no sign of him so she went back to their hotel alone.

The ball was the final event of the conference, and Martine had been looking forward to it, but she could not face going, not after last night; on impulse she picked up the phone and rang the airport.

Yes, there was a plane for London that evening; yes, there was a free seat on it. Martine booked herself on the plane, then hurriedly packed her bags, wrote a note to Bruno, and went down to check out.

Two hours later she was in the air on the way home.

*　　*　　*

She woke up next morning with a splitting headache and a temperature, so that she didn't have to lie to Charles when she rang him at home.

'I flew home a night early; I'm coming down with flu, started throwing up, and it's so hateful being ill in hotels. I didn't miss any of the conference, though, except the ball. And Bruno is there, to cover anything that does happen.'

Charles was very sympathetic. 'Don't worry about it. I think you did the right thing, I hate being ill in hotels myself.'

'How are you? Feeling any better?' she asked, reminded that he had been ill before they left. In fact, that was why Bruno had gone at all. Charles should have been with her. She broke off a sigh, in case he heard it. If she had gone with Charles, how differently she would feel now!

'I'll be back at work on Monday—I'm fine,' he said. 'Maybe you've caught the same bug I had? I hope I didn't give it to you. Have you got a headache?'

'Frightful one.' But she suspected it wasn't flu that was making her head ache, although as she had been sick several times that day she knew now that it hadn't only been her shamed revulsion over letting Bruno make love to her that had made her throw up the morning she woke up to find him gone leaving just a curt note behind.

'High temperature? Thirsty? Shivery?'

'All that.'

'It sounds like what I had. Well, one comfort is, it doesn't last long. Stay in bed and call a doctor, and don't come back to work until you're one hundred per cent again.'

'I won't. Charles, I left my conference notes with Bruno, he'll give them to you if you want them urgently, but it would be easier for you to read them after they've been typed up.'

'Forget about work, Martine,' Charles told her firmly. 'Just concentrate on getting well.'

By that evening she felt terrible; it was definitely flu and she stayed in bed, shivering under a thick winter duvet, dosed herself with aspirin and drank a lot of squash and orange juice and water. She didn't eat at all, couldn't keep anything down.

When she went back to work she had lost weight and looked pale. Charles gave her a concerned look as she walked into his office.

'You have been ill! You look terrible.'

She laughed. 'Thank you, Charles, you're so flattering. Did Bruno give you my conference notes? Have they been typed up?'

'Yes, I've skimmed through them.' He talked about some of the topics which had been discussed at the conference, asked her some questions, then said, 'Guess who came into the office yesterday?'

Blankly, she said, 'Who?'

'Gerhard,' Charles said, laughing. 'He told me he'd run into you at the conference. He's in London with a team from Bundesbank to hold talks with the Bank of England. We're having lunch later this week—I told him I'd bring you along if you were back at work. Are you free on Thursday?'

'I think so. I'll have to check my diary, I'll let you know.'

She wasn't sure she wanted to see Gerhard again. Seeing him would always remind her now of what happened at the conference. Oh, that's so stupid, she thought! How could she forget any of it, when she still worked here, under the same roof as Bruno, and could hardly avoid seeing him every day?

And why on earth should she be so unfair towards Gerhard? It wasn't his fault, any of it. He didn't even know what had happened, nobody did. Red colour stained her face. She hoped nobody ever would.

She went to her own office to look at her diary and sat behind her desk, staring at nothing, wondering how she was going to feel when she finally saw Bruno again.

The phone rang; it was one of their investment managers, sounding gloomy. 'Martine, I'm having trouble with one of the clients—he's threatening to take his account away because he isn't satisfied with the way I'm managing his money. Could you talk to him? Have lunch with the two of us some time next week?'

She looked at her diary again, sighed. 'OK, Peter, Friday is free. Who is it?'

'His name's Weddon.'

'OK, send me his file down with all the details of the shares you've bought and how they're doing. I suppose we are making money for him?'

Peter droned apologetically, 'Well, I had one or two pieces of bad luck. You remember that big flotation we were handling in the spring—Brugell; I took up some of that for him. If you remember, we were all trying to talk clients into buying some.

And then, of course, it fell heavily not long afterwards.'

Martine's mouth indented. That had been one of their mistakes; they should never have got involved with that, but it had looked OK on the face of it.

'Why didn't you get rid of the shares for him? Switch into something else?'

'You know that's not our policy; Charles likes us to ride the ups and downs, not keep buying and selling. That was my instruction, and I stick to it.'

Martine made a face. 'Yes, Peter, but there are exceptions to that rule, and one of them is when a company is being run by crooks, and you know very well that Brugell's chairman has absconded with a lot of the company money. Well, I'll look at what you've been doing, and see if I can improve on our performance. Look, fix this lunch for next week, not this—that will give me more time to make some rearrangements.'

She rang off, and settled down to study the Japanese stock market, which was edgy at the moment, checking all the shares they held; comparing prices, the way the share had performed that year, on graphs held in their computer's memory. She had an appointment with a Japanese client that afternoon and wanted to be sure she knew what she was talking about.

It was lunchtime before she saw Bruno. She was walking out of the beautiful early-nineteenth-century building which housed the bank when Bruno strode towards her from a taxi which had just dropped him.

They met on the steps. Martine grasped the elegant ironwork railings for support, her heart lurching as she saw him.

His face was dark and cool; he nodded. 'Back at work, then?'

'Yes.'

'Charles said it was flu.' The sardonic tone said he didn't believe it.

She lifted her chin. 'Yes, that's right.' Her own tone told him she didn't care what he believed.

His mouth twisted cynically. 'But now you're back to normal.'

Anyone else overhearing them would have taken what he said at face value, but Martine heard the undertone, the sarcasm and distaste, and flinched from it.

'Yes,' she said, staring bitterly into his black eyes.

'I know you'll be pleased to hear that Charles kept saying how much he missed you,' he drawled. 'They say absence makes the heart grow fonder, don't they? So your bout of flu was brilliantly timed, obviously.'

She didn't answer, her face stiff, just walked away, blinded to the traffic and confusion of London through which she moved. She hadn't seen him for more than a week, but he had never been out of her mind all that time, and, just now, while they talked, she had kept looking at him, looking away, unable to stop looking back, swinging wildly all the time between extremes of feeling which left her giddy.

Absence had had a drastic effect on her heart, it seemed. She wished to God it hadn't.

That brief encounter on the steps outside the cream-washed façade of the bank would make it easier next time she saw him, though. She hoped.

In fact, she saw him again the following day, in Charles's office. There were several of the bank's directors there; Martine and Bruno were able to ignore each other most of the time without it seeming strange.

Nobody else seemed to notice the chill in the air whenever they spoke to each other, either, although it seemed so obvious to Martine. Only Charles picked up on it, and mentioned it later, in private, gently chiding her.

'What is it with you and Bruno? I hoped you two would get on better than you obviously do. Didn't you hit it off while you were in Rome? I thought that being thrown together like that might have broken the ice between you, but the way you talk to each other lately the ice seems thicker than ever.'

Flushed, and furious with herself for letting Charles glimpse her feelings she said huskily, 'I'm sorry if it's that obvious. I always try to be polite.'

'Oh, polite, yes. But I know you both, I don't need you to draw diagrams. Every time the two of you are in the same room the temperature goes down with a thump. You know my plans for him, Martine—one day he'll be sitting in my chair. Try to make friends with him.'

She forced a pretence of laughter. 'Good heavens, Charles, stop talking as if you're ninety-three! Unless you're planning to retire at fifty, Bruno isn't going to take over for a long, long time.'

Then their eyes met and she frowned, struck by a new idea.

'You aren't planning to retire, are you?' That prospect appalled her. Charles, gone. Bruno in his place? She would have to leave the bank!

'I'm certainly not planning anything of the kind, but you never know what the future holds, do you? So make friends with Bruno, Martine.'

It was too late for that, she thought grimly. She and Bruno were never going to be friends. They had briefly been lovers—now they were enemies.

CHAPTER FIVE

NOVEMBER was a grey and drizzly month; skeletal leaves blew along the windswept pavements and people looked fed up as they hurried in and out of offices and shops. Bruno jetted off to Australia and New Zealand on a fact-finding mission to have meetings with investment managers across the continent, clients of the bank who lived there, and to get an inside look at the Australian stock market, the major companies and growth areas. All world markets were volatile; the Australian one was no exception and you couldn't really get an idea of what was happening to it from this side of the globe.

Martine was working late the night before he left. Everyone else had gone home, but she had to finish some research on a new investment programme they were working out for a big pension fund.

She stopped to massage her eyes, Chinese style; her elbows on her desk and her palms pressed into her eyes, shutting out the light and easing the strain on the iris, at the same time letting her mind go blank. When she was very tired this often helped to revitalise her for a while.

She was totally unaware of Bruno's approach until he touched her shoulder.

Then she whirled round, green eyes wide in shock.

'Oh! It's you! Don't creep up on me like that, you nearly made my heart stop.'

'And we wouldn't want that, would we?' he said drily, and she felt herself flush. You had to be on your toes when you talked to him; he used double meanings like thorns under the skin. She let that one go by without comment.

'Why are you still working? You've got a long flight tomorrow, you should get an early night.'

'I shall,' he said. 'I'm just off, but I saw your light and came in to say goodbye. I'm sure you'll be relieved to see me go.'

She would, and yet she already felt a grey depression settling down over her like the mists of winter. She was going to miss him badly, but she wasn't admitting that to him.

One black brow curved sardonically. 'No comment? Well, none needed. But as I shall miss the Christmas office party and all the fun and games under the mistletoe which I understand goes on . . .' He bent very fast, before she had time to realise what he intended, and kissed her, his lips hot, compelling, waking the sleeping passion always coiled inside her body whenever he was near her.

It only lasted a moment, then he stood up, breathing thickly, darkly flushed, his eyes hostile.

'You can slap my face when I get back! Don't marry Charles while I'm away or you'll be very sorry you did,' he said, and walked out, leaving her trembling, frustrated, on the point of tears.

After he had gone it seemed to her to rain every day, and she couldn't get him out of her mind, especially at night, in her bed, when erotic fantasies about him kept her awake for hours.

'Lucky Bruno,' Charles said, looking out of the window one morning when the rain was beating down outside. 'If it weren't for the exhausting flight I'd have gone myself, but I couldn't face the journey.'

'I've never been to Australia,' she wistfully said.

'You should have said something! You could have gone with Bruno.'

'I didn't want to!' she erupted, caught Charles's eye and flushed. 'Well, you wouldn't want us both to be away at the same time, would you!'

Charles frowned. 'That's true. But, I've just realised—you can't stand him, can you? Odd; I find him likeable; a brilliant mind, too, very shrewd. I wonder why you don't like him?'

'I can't like everyone!' she protested, then tried to change the subject. 'Weather likes this makes you think of holidays somewhere hot and sunny, doesn't it? The Caribbean would be nice! Or Florida.'

'How about Germany?' Charles said wryly, and she gave him a startled look.

'Germany? That's not sunny! I remember Gerhard telling me about winters there when he was a child, how he skied to school and went skating on frozen lakes.'

'Yes, I know—but Gerhard did invite us to visit the Bundesbank and the diary is pretty empty for the start of December.'

Martine thought about it, chewing the end of a pen. 'Both of us?'

Charles looked mischievous. 'I think Gerhard would expect you to be there! Don't you?'

She grinned. 'I don't know what you mean!'

'Oh, yes, you do. He fancies you.' Charles lifted an eyebrow. 'Come on, you know you like him.'

'Of course I do.' And it was true that the first ten days of December was a blank space in her diary. Later there would be a lot of Christmas parties, both private ones and office parties.

'And while we're over there, we could do some Christmas shopping,' Charles said cheerfully. 'After we've had our discussions with Gerhard at the Bundesbank we could stay on for a couple of days and go to one of the wonderful Christmas fairs they have in Germany at this time of year.'

Her eyes lit up. 'Yes, that would be fun!'

'I suppose you'll be spending Christmas with your family as usual?'

'I'm not sure. I often do go home for Christmas, as well as for a week in the summer. It's much too far to go home at weekends, I'd no sooner get there than I'd have to drive back, so I like to have at least a week at home when I do go.'

'Do they come to London often? Where do they go for their holidays?' Charles was always interested in other people's lives; it was one of the things about him that made him a good boss and a good friend.

Martine sighed. 'My father hasn't had a day off in years. He's too bound up with life on the farm; he works three hundred and sixty-five days in the year, and so does my mother.'

Martine kept trying to persuade her parents to come to London, or to come away with her, on a foreign holiday in some exotic country, but it never happened.

The family hill farm, in the border lands between England and Scotland, made very little money, but her father loved it dearly. He was happy getting up before the sun broke through, looking after stock, mending dry stone walls, hedging and ditching, injecting sheep against the dozen or so diseases they were prone to, doing any of the hundreds of jobs which needed doing on the farm at any time of the year.

Joe Archer had been a big man in his youth; now he stooped but he was still tall, very wiry, with weathered brown skin, dark red hair thick with grey now, and brown eyes. His had been a hard life, but it was the life he had chosen for himself, and he never regretted it, never complained.

Martine's mother never complained, either, or gave any sign of resentment for the toughness of her daily life. She worked just as hard as her husband, indoors and out. She made the bread they ate, fed the hens and collected their eggs, killed them too, and cooked them. She washed the clothes and linen; she ironed and baked and scrubbed and cleaned.

There was never any money, and that had been a spur to Martine's own ambition. She had soon understood that if she wanted to get on in life she had to get good results at school. She had worked with intense concentration and got the results she needed. She had chosen banking as a career because she hadn't wanted to teach, enter the law, or any other possible profession, but her mother's brother had been a local bank manager and had told her banking was a good career for a girl these days.

So she had come down to London and got a first job here, in the bank, rising with surprising speed as she realised what an aptitude she had for the work. She found it all so fascinating: the big companies, share movements, commodity broking, the swings and roundabouts of money; the ups and downs of the dollar, the Deutschmark, the pound, the yen, the franc. She loved the speed of transactions, the electrifying nervous tension of the market on either good days or bad. Banking might sound dull to someone who only understood the day-to-day routine of a local bank, but to anyone working in a busy merchant bank it could be as exciting as love; as dangerous as piracy on the high seas, as nerve-racking as fighting to the death.

As the years went by she had grown away from her parents to some extent. She loved her father, but she had never felt able to relax with him. He had tunnel vision; only saw life from one point of view. She couldn't talk to him; he had no idea about the world she inhabited, the sort of life she led, and she was bored by talk of sheep disease, mineral deficiency in the grass, the price of lamb on the open market. They had nothing much in common any more, except shared blood.

He wouldn't even accept her offer to help financially when she knew times were hard for them. However much Martine assured them she could afford to send them money every month, her father refused to take it.

'You keep your money for yourself, girl!' was all he said. After years of living on a remote hill farm, where little from the outside world penetrated, he had a rigid, old-fashioned attitude to life. His pride wouldn't let him take money from his daughter. He might have taken it from a son, but never from a girl.

When Martine secretly sent money to her mother, Joe Archer made his wife send it back, and Marie Archer had written a short note with it asking Martine not to do that again.

Joe Archer lived by fixed ideas, fixed moral standards he had learnt in his youth. He read no newspapers, had no TV, rarely even listened to the radio. Martine knew that her parents lived in a sort of time-warp where nothing had altered since 1940; for instance, her father would be deeply shocked if he ever found out that she had slept with Bruno; he probably believed she was still a virgin at twenty-seven, waiting for the right man to come along before she married.

Her mother was a gentle, tolerant woman, but she had never supported Martine against her father in the past, and Martine didn't expect she ever would. Marie Archer was the sort of wife who said, 'My husband, right or wrong...' and stuck to it. Nearly sixty now, she looked older. The auburn hair she had passed on to her daughter had turned grey; her face had too many lines, and she always seemed tired.

Martine saw how the long hours of hard work were sapping her mother's strength, turning her old before her time, and each time she went home she had to bite her tongue not to say anything to her father, because her interference only upset her mother and never achieved anything. The truth was, her parents had shared everything, throughout their marriage; there was a deep, quiet love between them which had never altered, and never would.

So, it was better for her to go home very infrequently; she could hold her tongue if she rarely saw them.

'I've always thought I'd love to spend Christmas somewhere really romantic, like Vienna,' she idly said.

'We'll, why don't you?' said Charles. 'I'd like to go to Vienna for Christmas too. We could go together.'

She gave him a startled look, laughed. 'It would be magical, wouldn't it?' She didn't take him seriously; she thought that, like her, he was only fantasising, daydreaming. She had seen a programme on TV about Vienna the other day, had been enchanted by the wonderful architecture, the Belvedere Palace, the Schoenbrunn palace, Vienna cathedral, the State Opera House, and moved by the music that had surged behind the voice-over; Mozart, the waltzes of the Strauss family, but most of all by the sight of bell-decked horses pulling sleighs through the snowy Vienna woods on a winter's day.

'Let's do it,' Charles urged, and she suddenly realised he meant it.

He met her eyes, his face coaxing. 'I hate Christmas on my own. Friends invite me but family Christmas always makes me feel melancholy.

Staying in hotels is even worse, all that fake jollity and gaudy paper hats, waiters dressing up as Father Christmas! But you and me...we both know the score, we're just good friends, and no complications on either side. So, what do you say, Martine? Will you come?'

There was something so wistful about his tone; she hesitated, then threw caution to the winds and nodded recklessly. 'OK, let's do it.'

They sat and planned it there and then, and Martine went out to book the trip the following day. They would fly out three days before Christmas and come back a week later, stay in one of the best hotels in Vienna. They were both excited—it brightened the wintry days that followed, like candles burning in a dark place.

But that was before it dawned on her that she had missed two periods. She hadn't worried much about the lateness of the first one; she had never had regular periods. But she had never gone two months before, and as the days went by and nothing happened she began to be scared.

What if...but it couldn't be! Bruno had taken precautions; she couldn't be going to have his baby.

But if not, what was wrong with her? She was afraid to go to her doctor, a rather stuffy middle-aged man who didn't look as if he might be very sympathetic.

It would be so embarrassing to tell him she thought she might be pregnant; so she went to a chemist and bought a do-it-yourself pregnancy test. The instructions were very complicated and she hated having to go through the process; but she couldn't rest until she knew, so she did it at once that evening.

The result was positive. She sat looking at it with a white face and dark, shadowy eyes.

She was carrying Bruno's baby. Her stomach clenched in sick protest and dismay. Oh, why had she been so reckless and stupid? This was a consequence she hadn't been expecting. She had kept telling herself that, much as she bitterly regretted losing her head like that, at least she didn't have to worry about getting pregnant. How could she possibly have expected to be the one in a million for whom the precautions did not work?

In the first shock of the realisation she couldn't decide what to do. Her first thought was to have an abortion; the sooner the better. But she was afraid, and undecided. She couldn't make up her mind about something so drastic and terrifying in such a hurry. She needed time to think.

Should she have the child, but let it be adopted? Oh, but the very thought of going through a pregnancy, while working at the bank, and everyone knowing what was happening to her body, made her feel sick, especially because it would mean that Bruno would know.

She had no intention of telling him until she couldn't avoid it. This was her body; the decision had to be hers. He had no rights in the baby at all, she told herself bitterly, not after the way he had behaved.

While she was still trying to make up her mind what to do, she and Charles flew to Frankfurt late in November to have a series of meetings with

Gerhard and a handful of other top German bank executives. They had a heavy agenda; as usual the thorny topic of German interest rates and the European Common Market monetary practice was head of the list of subjects they discussed. There was no hope of changing German policy on that, but these inter-bank contacts were always useful in creating the right atmosphere for future development.

When the business of the day was over, though, Gerhard showed them Frankfurt's night life.

They were staying in the Frankfurter Hof, a grand hotel of the type Charles most enjoyed; each evening Gerhard arrived in a chauffeur-driven limousine to take them out to dinner and dance.

Charles tired early, and always suggested that Martine should stay on later, but she wouldn't hear of that. 'I have to get up early, too,' she would protest and go back to the hotel with him when he went. For Charles the best night was the one when Gerhard took them to the City Opera at the arts complex on Theaterplatz. Charles managed to stay awake for that, but on their last night in Frankfurt he went to bed early and didn't come out at all.

Gerhard took Martine to the latest disco to open in Frankfurt; they shouted at each other and danced in a darkness split every second by a revolving flash of coloured neon light, the heavy beat of the music raving around them.

Gerhard kissed her in the car on the way back to her hotel, and murmured huskily, 'Can I come in tonight?'

She had been expecting the question ever since they arrived, which was why she had always avoided being alone with him after Charles went to bed.

She stiffened in his arms, very flushed. 'I . . . I'm sorry, Gerhard . . . no.'

He looked down at her, his eyes intent. 'Do you mean not tonight? Or never, Martine?'

'I like you, Gerhard, you know that, I find you very attractive and charming, you've been a wonderful host, I've really enjoyed our visit here . . .'

'But . . . ?' he said drily.

She couldn't meet his eyes.

'There's someone else?' he asked and she hesitated, then nodded. 'I think I can guess,' Gerhard said.

Her green eyes lifted in shock.

Gerhard smiled crookedly at her. 'Bruno Falcucci, isn't it? I picked up vibes between the two of you in Rome.'

She flinched. Had it been so obvious?

'It was like being caught in an electrical storm; I almost ducked once or twice,' Gerhard drawled. 'But I wasn't sure whether you hated him or loved him, so I thought . . .' He shrugged with wry sophistication. 'What do you say in England . . . nothing venture, nothing gain? You're beautiful and clever, I rarely meet girls I find as attractive as I find you.'

She blushed and said shyly, 'Thank you, Gerhard. I like you, too, you know.'

'That's nice. I'll try to feel comforted by that thought,' he said wryly. 'Well, no hard feelings, Martine. I've really enjoyed showing you and

Charles around Frankfurt, I hope you come back soon, and I'll certainly be over in London some time in the new year. And who knows, if you and Bruno never get it together, there might still be a happy ending for me?'

Marten was shaken, staring at him. 'Gerhard, I don't know what to say.' She had been expecting him to make a pass, but she hadn't for an instant supposed he might be serious about her. Was he saying that he was?

He gave her one of his charming, dry smiles. 'Don't look at me like a wounded fawn, Martine. My heart isn't broken. I'll live.'

They arrived at the Frankfurter Hof and Gerhard kissed her hand lingeringly. 'It has been a magical interlude; thank you, Martine.'

For some stupid reason, tears filled her eyes. 'You're so kind, Gerhard, you've made our trip here so wonderful.' She hugged him, gave a husky sob, and ran into the hotel.

She lay awake half the night thinking that if she had never met Bruno she might have fallen in love with Gerhard and been very happy with him. It was another reason why she hated Bruno. He had blighted her life in so many ways.

She and Charles left for the airport early in the morning. Martine was pale and strained; she had a headache and felt queasy on the airport bus. She was afraid for a time that she was going to throw up. Charles kept looking at her anxiously as they waited in the check-in queue.

'Are you sure you aren't coming down with something? You look terrible, Martine.'

'Too many late nights,' she said lightly.

The queue seemed to be crawling along. They had been standing there for ten minutes; she wished she could sit down, she felt so strange.

'Martine...' she heard Charles say from far away and that was the moment when she realised she was going to faint.

She crumpled up without a sound, her auburn hair tumbling around her white face.

They called the airport doctor and Martine was taken, protesting, to a quiet room where the doctor examined her and asked her questions which Charles translated for her, then translating her replies.

After a few moments, Charles asked, 'He wants to know if there have been any other symptoms?'

Martine swallowed, biting her inner lip.

Her hesitation didn't escape the doctor, who asked Charles something sharply.

Charles gave her a quick, startled look, then said, 'He says... could you be pregnant?'

Martine didn't meet his eyes. She nodded.

Charles didn't have to translate that. The doctor smiled, said, 'Ah!' and added a flow of quick German which Charles, also, did not translate.

'He says that that is the probable explanation for the faint, then,' Charles quietly said. 'If you have any further problems you should see your own doctor as soon as you get home.'

They left the doctor and walked through the busy, echoing airport without speaking; bought newspapers, magazines, which they read while they waited to board their plane. On the flight Martine avoided meeting Charles's eyes, and he was grimly silent, his face absorbed.

It wasn't until they were back in London and driving back through the rainy city that Charles asked in a low voice, pitched so that the driver should not hear him, 'When is it due?'

She didn't want to answer, but after a pause she muttered, 'June.'

Charles was silent for a moment; she could almost hear him thinking, then he said, 'Have you made any plans yet? Will you marry the father?'

She shook her head, staring out of the window, her pale profile rigid.

She hoped Charles would stop asking questions, but he quietly went on, 'Wasn't it serious, Martine? Just a brief affair, was that it?'

She laughed, suddenly bitterly angry. 'Brief is the understatement of the year. It was one night, that's all, and this had to happen! Life is unfair!'

Charles looked stunned. No doubt he was shocked; he himself was not a man given to promiscuity and she sensed that he hadn't imagined she would be, either. Useless now to protest that it had been wildly out of character, that she had never intended it to happen, that she bitterly regretted it.

'Does the father know?' asked Charles and she shook her head. 'Will you tell him?' he asked and she shook her head again.

Another long silence, then, 'Do I know him?' Charles asked, and she hesitated a fraction of a second too long. 'I do,' Charles said before she could answer, then, too fast for her to see it coming, 'Is it Bruno?'

Her head swung, and she looked at him in white-faced disbelief. How had he leapt to that conclusion? She hadn't given him any clues that she could remember. First Gerhard had guessed, now Charles. Was she really so obvious?

Charles's mouth indented and he frowned. 'You were always a little too extreme in your reactions to him,' he explained his shrewd guesswork, on a sigh. 'I wondered what you really felt, and then, when you both came back from Rome there was something different between you—I knew something had happened there. The air turned glacial every time you were in the same room.'

She leaned back in the car, turning away to hide the gleam of tears in her eyes. Charles was so sensitive, so perceptive. Why couldn't Bruno be more like him?

When they reached her flat Charles said, 'I'll see you safely upstairs,' and murmured something to his driver in an aside too low for her to hear. As they entered the building, she heard the limousine drive off and looked round, looked up at Charles, frowning.

'Why have you sent your driver away?'

'I want to talk to you. I'll take a taxi home.'

Weariness in her voice, she said, 'Charles, please, I don't feel up to talking about this tonight. I'll sort my problem out and let you know what I plan to do, later this week.'

Charles ignored her protest, following her into her flat. 'Let me make you a hot drink—how about cocoa or hot milk?'

She put a hand to her mouth, nauseated by the mention of the drinks, ran to the bathroom.

When she came back she apologised. 'At the moment, anything seems to make me throw up.'

'You poor girl, sit down. I've made some tea,' Charles said. He had explored her kitchen and found some crackers too, and made her eat one. They sat and sipped their tea together in silence. It was very weak, a straw-coloured liquid.

'Have you decided yet whether you're going to have the baby or not?' asked Charles and she shook her head.

'I've been trying to make up my mind for weeks, ever since I found out.'

'Do you want to keep it? Will your family help you?'

She laughed grimly. 'I have no intention of telling them, even if I do keep it. My father would never speak to me again; he isn't broad-minded, he would be ashamed of me, he would be afraid everyone he knew would find out and gossip about me. He's lived in an isolated country area all his life; they don't even have a TV, I offered to give them one for Christmas one year and he refused, didn't like the idea. It was too new-fangled for him. He hasn't had a new idea in his head since he was in his teens, I suspect.'

Charles was fascinated. 'What about your mother?'

'She would never argue with my father. What he says goes, in our house. He's not a violent man, he never raised his hand to me, but he won't stand for being contradicted, especially by a woman.'

'He sounds monstrous,' Charles said, looking appalled.

She gave a little groan of bleak amusement. 'No, he's just a narrow-minded man who has never adjusted to changing morality. I shan't be asking my parents for any help or support.'

There was a long silence, then Charles said quietly, 'I've got news of my own for you, Martine. I'm under sentence of death.'

She almost dropped the cup she held. Her hand shaking, she carefully put the cup down, staring at him. 'What are you talking about?'

'I have a brain tumour,' he said in a casual, down-to-earth voice which made it even harder to take in what he was telling her. 'They say it's inoperable, and growing worse.'

Numbly, she kept her eyes fixed on his face, unable to believe it, yet reading the truth of it in every detail of the way he looked. Charles was so heartbreakingly thin now; his hair had no life in it, there were more silver strands every day and his skin was waxen, drawn too tightly across his fine bone-structure. He was beginning to look as skeletal as one of the leaves blowing through the London streets in the winter rain.

'Oh, Charles,' she whispered, her lips quivering.

'I could have six months, I could have six days,' he said calmly. 'They can't give me any definite answers. Now you see why I suddenly sent for Bruno and offered him a top job at the bank. I have no children, my wife and I never managed to have any before . . .' His voice wavered at last. 'Before she died.'

Hearing the pain in his voice, for his wife, which was not there for himself, tears welled up in Martine's eyes. 'Charles, darling Charles,' she said brokenly, and knelt down beside his chair, put her head on his lap, her arms around his waist, feeling as she held him how painfully thin he was, how frail and fleshless. She broke out angrily. 'Why is life so unfair? Why do these things happen?'

He stroked her rich auburn hair with a gentle hand. 'I asked myself those questions when I had that crash, and killed Elizabeth. I'd have given my own life to save hers, yet I was the one who killed her. It was such cruel irony. I never got an answer, and I still don't have one. These things do happen out of the blue to anyone, without rhyme or reason, and it's no use complaining that they're unfair.'

She was silent for a minute, then asked huskily, 'Are you absolutely sure there's no chance of an operation? Wouldn't it be worth taking a risk?'

Charles shrugged. 'They have told me frankly that there is almost no chance of them being able to remove the tumour without killing me. And I've been rushing ever since to put my affairs in order. If I had died a few months back, when they first suspected the tumour, I would have left chaos behind me. I hadn't made proper provision about anything; my wife's death invalidated my only will and I had some serious decisions to make. Now, I've tidied things up, and one of my decisions was to bring Bruno over to London and put him into a position at the bank where he could get to know the business before I died and he inherited all my shares.'

She frowned suddenly. 'Have you told him? Does Bruno know you're so ill?'

He shook his head. 'You're the only person I've told, apart from my specialists and my own doctor. Bruno has no idea.'

'But he does know you've made a will, leaving everything to him, all the shares in the bank?'

Charles shook his head again. 'No. And after what you've just told me I've had second thoughts. I need an heir to carry on at the bank after me, and you need a father for your baby. The child will have my blood in its veins, after all; it seems a very neat solution to both our problems, don't you agree? So, Martine, will you marry me?'

She almost thought for a minute that she hadn't heard him correctly, and she didn't answer, just looked blankly at him. He stared back, a half-smile curling his pale mouth, his blue eyes wry and gentle.

'Will you marry me, Martine?' he repeated then, watching the expressions flick across her incredulous white face. 'At once,' he added. 'And don't spend too long considering my proposal. There's no time to lose, for either of us.'

CHAPTER SIX

MARTINE didn't even need to think for a second. Shaking her head in utter disbelief, she whispered, 'Charles...thank you...you're the kindest man I know, and that's the most wonderful offer...you've taken my breath away, and I'll never forget that you asked me, but, you know, I couldn't possibly accept.'

'Why not?' He seemed taken aback, as if he had expected her to jump at his proposal.

She made a husky sound, half sob, half laughter. 'Dear Charles, I couldn't marry you for your money, even if it *was* all intended for my baby. I couldn't live with myself if I did. No, it's very sweet and thoughtful of you to want to help me, but money isn't really the answer to my problems. I earn enough to be able to take care of my baby myself, after all, and I have plenty of savings put by. I shall work something out after the birth, find someone to look after the baby while I work. Lots of other women find themselves in this predicament and manage to cope, I'm sure I shall, once I put my mind to it. And, as for you needing an heir with your family blood in his veins, well, I can't advise you on that, but Bruno is still your nearest relative and he understands merchant banking better than anyone I know apart from you.'

111

She got up, pushing back her slightly dishevelled auburn hair with both hands and Charles got to his feet too, frowning.

'I thought you hated him.'

She laughed. 'The way I feel about him doesn't stop me assessing his abilities honestly and recognising that the man is brilliant!'

'Yes, he is, isn't he?' Charles murmured, pushing his hands into his pockets and rocking on the balls of his feet. 'Brilliant, but amoral, it seems. I'm not sure that makes him a suitable candidate to take my chair at the bank, Martine. I'm not someone who believes you don't need a morality if you're in banking.'

'I'm sure Bruno has very high ethical standards where banking is concerned,' she drily told him, and Charles grinned at her, his face lightening.

'You can always make me laugh, even when I'm very down. And you're astonishingly fair-minded. I don't think many girls, in your shoes, would have been so strictly scrupulous where Bruno was concerned.'

She couldn't quite meet his eyes. In a low, muffled voice she said, 'He didn't force me to do anything I didn't want to do, you know.'

Charles was silent but he took her hand and held it tightly, comforting her without words.

'I may hate his guts,' she went on with bitter humour, 'but he didn't make me any promises, he didn't cheat me or lie to me. We didn't even have an affair; I think Gerhard put it in a nutshell...'

'Gerhard?' Charles repeated, looking astounded. 'He knows about the baby?'

'No, but he did guess that I'd been involved with Bruno. He said being with the two of us was like being caught in an electrical storm.'

Charles laughed. 'He hit the button there! I know exactly what he means.'

'Well, the one time we made love was like being hit by lightning, but getting up and walking away feeling dazed. I still don't know why I let it happen. But it's personal, Charles, just between me and Bruno. Don't let what happened between me and him make any difference to you. I'll admit, I never trusted Bruno, from the start, but if I'd known you were so ill I wouldn't have been quite so suspicious of him, I think. The point was, I thought you were being premature, sending for him to join the bank, talking of making him your heir. I thought you were much too young for all that, but that Bruno might take advantage of you. You were only running on one cylinder all these months, and Bruno was taking over right in front of my eyes. Now I understand what was behind your thinking and I have to admit, you've made the best possible choice, as far as the bank is concerned. He's streets ahead of any other candidates to take over from you.'

Charles listened carefully, nodding. 'I agree. He is. But it's very generous of you to say so, all the same. You're a remarkable woman, Martine. I should have thought of proposing to you long ago. I wonder what you would have said, if I had?'

There was a curious, questioning tone in his voice; she smiled at him affectionately. 'More or less what I said just now, Charles. I'm very fond of you and I admire you, but marriage should be based on something more substantial than that.'

'You're right, of course,' he said, his mouth rueful. 'That's why I never married until I met Elizabeth. It's true I was always busy, but even so I met enough women during those years, some of them very attractive. The fact was, I simply didn't meet anyone I wanted to spend my life with, and it bothered me for a long time. I thought I might be frigid, emotionally cold, incapable of loving anyone. Then I finally found Elizabeth and fell for her like a ton of bricks.' His eyes were full of pain. 'She was the most wonderful thing that ever happened to me, Martine; since I lost her I haven't really cared whether I lived or died.'

'Maybe that's why you...' Martine began then broke off.

He looked down at her, brows arching. 'Maybe why I what?'

'Got the tumour,' she whispered reluctantly, and Charles gave her a slightly irritated frown.

'You think I'm imagining it? I wish I were!'

'No, of course not,' she protested. 'But sometimes we can make ourselves ill when we're very unhappy.'

He thought about that. 'The tumour might be psychosomatic, you mean? I don't know, but it exists, Martine. I've seen the X-rays. Only a little of it is visible, the bulk of it is hidden, and inaccessible, they just know it's there; there's enough to see for the doctors to be certain it's large, and growing.'

'Charles, I'm sure the thing exists, but that's the whole point; the mind and the body are so closely entwined that they interact on each other all the time. Unhappiness can take strange forms, some of them actually physical.'

'I wouldn't wish myself a fatal brain tumour!' he said impatiently. 'I have such terrible headaches, and I'm having serious problems with my eyes—that's how they realised what was wrong, the eye problems. I began to think I was going blind; part of my field of vision had gone on my left side.'

She was aghast. 'You never said a word! How long has that been happening?'

'It's been gradual, and some days it's worse than others. Why do you think I've had so much time off work in the last few months? I stayed at home when it was really bad. Martine, nobody in their right minds would voluntarily go through what I have.'

'Charles, I'm so sorry,' she said, wrenched with sympathy. 'I wish you'd told me sooner; you shouldn't have coped with all this on your own!'

He shrugged, said wryly, 'You would have told me it was all psychological!'

Stricken, she broke out, 'That wasn't what I've been saying! Believe me, I wasn't implying that you knowingly wanted to have a brain tumour, but...you did just say that you didn't care whether you lived or died!'

His face changed, stiffened in a sort of shock. 'Yes, but...' He broke off, his eyes confused and troubled. 'My God, that never occurred to me. Do you really think I might have unconsciously invited it—that's what you're saying, isn't it? That my own mind has made this thing grow in my brain?'

'Not consciously, Charles,' she hurriedly said. 'Look, I can't understand why the hospital hasn't offered you counselling—you should be talking to someone about this, some sort of therapist who is used to dealing with these situations. Why don't you ask your doctor to recommend somebody?'

He shrugged. 'Oh, they suggested I saw someone like that, several times, but I couldn't see the point. I could accept death, I didn't need to be talked into accepting it.'

She was appalled. Her face urgent and distressed, she said, 'But don't you see, that's just the point? You accepted death too easily, you were half willing it. You need counselling badly, Charles. Please go and see someone at once, fix it up first thing tomorrow.'

He looked almost sulky. 'I still don't see that there's any point.'

'Of course there is,' she said, on the verge of tears again. 'I don't want you to die, Charles! I'd miss you terribly, we all would. You're far too young to give up on life like this.'

He looked touched. 'That's very sweet of you, Martine, but——'

'Don't say but!' She grabbed his shoulders and shook him. 'Charles, you must start fighting. You can't just let this horrible thing in your head win!'

He gave her a rueful look. 'You've always been a fighter, Martine. I spotted it in you the minute I met you, when you were as green as grass and just out of business college. I was a fighter, too, once. I don't know if I have the energy now.'

'Find some!' she told him fiercely. 'Charles, try anything, don't just sit around here waiting to die!'

He looked confused, his face full of shifting emotions, thoughts, uncertainties.

'When they first told me, I think I did just accept it,' he conceded at last. 'It seemed . . . like fate. I was too miserable to care. To be fair to them, there was talk of possible treatment, if an operation never became possible—they say that sometimes the tumour moves into a new area, where they can operate, and they're waiting to see if that happens. I asked them to give it to me straight, not wrap it up. I wanted to know what my chances were, and when they said I might only have a few weeks, or months, I told them I didn't want any of these new-fangled treatments that might not even work. They use lasers, I think. I didn't listen to any of that.'

'Well, go back and ask them to do something. Try any avenue, Charles—don't just give in!'

'It's probably too late now . . .'

She groaned, shaking him again. 'Don't be so defeatist! At least try!'

He looked down at her and gave that charming, boyish smile she had always loved. 'OK, OK, I'll ring tomorrow.' Then he said softly: 'Was I wrong, or have you definitely made up your mind to have this baby and keep it?'

She sighed. 'I don't know. At first, when I was in shock, I did think of an abortion, but I can't quite bring myself to do it.'

Charles listened without comment; she gave him a wry smile.

'You can't escape your upbringing, can you? My father brought me up to face my own responsibility for what I've done, not just get rid of the evidence and try to walk away as if nothing had happened. Abortion would be ducking out, wouldn't it?'

'It's your body—you're the one who has to decide. Women have abortions every day,' said Charles dispassionately.

'Yes, I know,' she said slowly. 'And I respect their reasons for coming to that decision; they have other circumstances to cope with, other backgrounds. I only know how I feel. I'm the one who has to live with the consequences, whichever way I take, all because I was reckless and stupid for just one night and went to bed with Bruno.'

'You see the baby as a punishment you deserve?' Charles thought aloud. 'What about the child, though? If you aren't going to want it, if you feel resentful, it seems a pretty grim outlook for the baby.'

Martine gave him a stricken stare. 'I hadn't thought about it from the baby's point of view! Oh, damn...why is everything so complicated? I'm only just beginning to come to terms with the idea that I'm pregnant, I'm still seeing everything from my own angle. Don't confuse me even more, Charles! Maybe we both need counselling!'

He laughed involuntarily. 'I think we do. Aren't we a pathetic pair? But you can always allow the child to be adopted, Martine, after the birth.'

She felt a strange, angry clutch in her stomach and her green eyes flashed. 'No, I shall keep it,' she said, realising that without being aware of the fact she had already decided on that.

'I suppose the maternal instinct is the basic female instinct!' Charles said in an approving voice, and she gave him a half-irritated look.

'Don't talk about instincts! It was a very basic instinct that got me into this mess in the first place!'

Charles laughed. 'Well, I think you'll make a good mother—you can be so calm and down-to-earth yet at the same time you're sympathetic and understanding. Lucky baby.'

Martine inwardly shivered. For the first time she actually wondered what the baby would be like if... when... it arrived; would it have her red hair and green eyes or would it inherit Bruno's colouring, black hair and eyes, an olive skin? And then she felt a stab of nervous tension and pushed the new ideas away. She didn't want to think that way. It made this baby too real, it made it harder for her to make a cool-headed, sensible decision about its future.

Charles glanced at his watch. 'I'd better be on my way, it's getting late. I'll pick up a taxi on the Embankment.' At the door, he paused. 'We are still going to Vienna, aren't we, Martine?'

She gave him a searching, uncertain look. 'Will you be well enough?'

His voice casual, he said, 'As long as this thing in my head doesn't suddenly start growing faster, I hope so. I'm living from day to day at the moment, but I really want to go, I'm looking forward to it enormously. It could be my last Christmas.'

She turned paler, flinched. 'Don't talk that way! Charles, you must stop being so negative; try to think positive thoughts.'

'Christmas in Vienna is a very positive thought,' he said, smiling at her. 'I have a feeling we will go! And I want it to be a very special time for both of us.' Then he paused, frowning, looked sharply at her. 'Unless you no longer want to go with me, now you know?' Dryness edged his tone. 'I shall understand if you feel you can't face the thought of spending a week on the edge of eternity.'

'Don't be silly, Charles! Of course I still want to go. I can't wait to see the Vienna woods in the snow,' she said at once, lightly, but after he had gone she felt her spirits sink, all her doubts and fears come back to haunt her.

That was yet another of her white nights. There had been so many nights like that lately, when she could not sleep, her mind going round and round, on the same old trails, like a mouse in a toy wheel. Tonight, though, she had something else to brood over. The bombshell of Charles's news was still reverberating inside her; the shock and grief kept growing, darkening, like a bruise which only came out on the skin as time went by.

What if he did die? She had worked with Charles ever since she came down to London from the North; she admired and loved him, she couldn't bear the thought of the bank without him.

She sat on her bed in white silk pyjamas, her knees up, her arms around them and her auburn

head propped up, staring into the dark, hearing rain
lash down the windows, the wind rattle a gate
somewhere. Out in the London streets the traffic
sounded like a distant roaring of animals, but
Martine was unaware of it, too accustomed to the
sound to hear it any more.

What Charles needed was to have some energy
and drive put into him to help him fight this thing
which was eating his brain away. Somehow she was
going to have to talk him into exerting himself—
saving his life, if he could. Charles must not simply
give in to death without a whimper. She wouldn't
let him.

Bruno returned from Australia a few days before
Christmas, to a London which was colder than it
had been so far that year. The thermometer had
dropped, and people began hopefully talking about
snow for Christmas.

Many of the offices in the bank were empty. One
group of staff were going on a skiing trip to
Switzerland organised by one of the young account
managers. Around a dozen members of staff were
going; mostly single, unattached people in their
twenties looking to have a good time with no strings
attached. Others were jetting off, singly, in pairs,
or small groups, to sunnier places, the Caribbean,
Florida, Tenerife; and Charles and Martine were
leaving the following day for Vienna.

When Bruno walked in she was busy clearing her
desk, making sure she had dealt with all corre-
spondence, going through client files to make sure
that everything was up to date before she left. It

wasn't an easy task because the phone kept ringing, and she was the only one around to answer it. Her secretary had taken the morning off to do some Christmas shopping.

Charles had an appointment with a Harley Street specialist. He had taken her advice; this was a trial appointment with a therapist, and he was very nervous about it.

When her office door opened she looked around, unsuspectingly, thinking it might be Charles back early, then felt her heart thud as she looked into Bruno's face.

'Hello, how are you?' he said, strolling into her office, letting the door close behind him, leaning on it, his arms folded, his long, lean body casually at ease.

'You're back,' Martine stupidly managed in a dry voice.

'I can tell you're thrilled to see me,' he mocked.

She ignored that. 'Did you have a good trip?'

'I learnt a lot,' he said, then drawled, 'When I walked through the bank, I had the feeling I'd stepped on to the Mary Celeste; every office seemed to be empty. Where is everybody?'

'Mostly gone away for Christmas,' Martine huskily managed to answer, unable to take her eyes off him. Seeing him again after this long interval made her realise how deeply she was in love; she drank in the sight of him as a thirsty man in a desert soaked up water.

His weeks in the Antipodes had given him a deep golden tan and it suited him. Usually he wore a suit to the office, but this morning, no doubt because it was almost Christmas and he was not expected back at work until after the festive season, he was wearing a white polo-neck sweater, blue denim jeans, a heavy sheepskin jacket, which he had taken off and held over one arm, not needing it in the centrally heated building.

'Has Charles gone away too?' he asked.

'No, Charles is . . .' She broke off, looked down, realising she had almost betrayed Charles's confidence. 'Out,' she finished.

Bruno's black brows arched. 'Are you and Charles the only people at work today?'

'No, of course not. I expect a lot of staff are doing Christmas shopping in their lunch-hour. For most of us this is our last day. Charles decided to give most people two weeks off at Christmas, although there will be a skeleton staff on duty every day. We worked out the rota long ago, don't you remember? I don't know how the rota affects you. By the way, we had the office party yesterday; I'm afraid you missed it.'

'I expect I shall survive the crushing disappointment,' he drily said, moving away from the door with the cool prowl of an animal stealthily making its way through its own, familiar jungle. 'Was it a good party?' he enquired, picking up some telex messages from her desk. 'Lots of drink and a few crisps and things on cocktail sticks?'

'It was fun,' she said, prickling at the way he watched her out of the corner of his eye. 'Clients dropped in, brought bottles with them. We put on music and danced.'

'Magic,' he said. 'Who did you dance with, or can I guess? Did Charles make it a romantic evening for you? How lucky I was away, I might have spoilt the rosy glow.'

'I'm sure you'd have done your best!' she snapped.

He laughed coldly. 'You can bet on it. So, where do you spend your Christmas? Have you got a family to go home to?'

'Well, I have, and I usually do go home for Christmas...'

'Where do your family live?'

'In the North,' she said, remembering that although he had been at school here for several years, and had visited the country frequently, he didn't really know Britain all that well, outside London and the South of England. 'In the borders, between Scotland and England,' she expanded. 'My family have farmed there for generations; it's nothing grand, just a little hill farm, with a couple of hundred acres of scrubby moorland full of gorse and heather. My father runs sheep and keeps a few pigs, goats and hens.' She was talking quickly, nervously, to stop him asking more personal questions.

He watched her, lounging against a chair now. His jeans were tight, she tried to stop her eyes wandering down over them, noticing the smooth line from waist to hip, the tension where the denim stretched over his thigh.

'Do you have brothers or sisters?' he asked curiously, and she shook her head.

'I was an only child.'

'Are you driving up there or taking a train?'

She hesitated, then had to say it. 'I'm not going home this Christmas, actually.'

She felt his alertness. 'What are you doing, then? You're not spending it alone in London?'

'No, we're going to Vienna,' she said in an offhand voice.

There was a silence. She looked sideways, her nerves jumping, but he was still leaning against the chair. His body was no longer casually at ease, though; it had tightened up, every muscle seeming poised for violent action, like the body of a runner before the gun went off. Suddenly the room was full of nervous tension and Bruno's dark eyes were molten.

'We?' he repeated. 'Who is we?'

'Me and Charles.'

'You and Charles are going to Vienna?' he asked in a controlled and quiet voice which made the hair rise on the back of her neck.

'Yes.' No word had ever been so hard to say.

'Just the two of you?' The voice was like the edge of a sword blade on the back of the neck, now.

'That's what I said! Yes!' she burst out, so jittery that she was angry. How dared he walk in here and cross-examine her as if this was a courtroom? She wasn't putting up with being terrorised, in her own office. Especially by a man who had no right to look at her as if she had committed some crime!

'You're going there on bank business?' he bit out, and she raised her chin at him, her green eyes stormy.

'I told you, we're spending Christmas there, in a hotel.'

She heard him breathing, on the other side of the room. 'You're going away for Christmas with Charles,' he repeated in what still sounded like a calm, cool voice, as though the idea was too difficult for him to take it in all at once.

'Yes!' she almost yelled, then closed her mouth on the rage mounting inside her. She must not let him get to her. Not again. But she couldn't sit still, she was too restless. She got up with an armful of folders, and walked over to the filing cabinets on the other side of the room. But that was a mistake too because Bruno's black eyes observed her every step, staring fixedly at her smoothly brushed auburn hair, the white silk shirt which clung to her breasts, the straight black jersey skirt which was a little tight and emphasised the instinctive sway of her hips, the hemline quite high, leaving bare her knees, her lower thighs, the long, slender, black-stockinged legs.

Martine had never been so conscious of her own body. She was having difficulty moving, breathing, thinking. She leaned weakly on the filing cabinet and began putting files away with hands that trembled.

'You *have* been busy while I was Down Under,' Bruno bit out.

She pretended to believe he was referring to the bank. 'You heard what a success the Filby take-over was? There was no real fight in their management, most shareholders accepted the Datoon offer and it's all over bar the shouting. Datoon were very happy with the way we managed things, but

Charles will tell you all about it when you talk to him later.'

'Will he tell me all about you and him, too?'

Blindly she reached for another file to slide into place, and suddenly Bruno was standing next to her.

She jumped, looking up in alarm. His eyes were black coals, angrily smouldering.

'Are you sleeping with him?'

'If I am, it's none of your business!'

'Look at me when you tell me that!' His hand shot out, caught her by the upper arm and pulled her round to face him.

Her green eyes frightened, but defiant, she gave him one brief glance, then looked down quickly, unable to hold his brooding stare.

'Let go of my arm!'

His hard fingers relaxed their grip on her, but did not let go. Instead they began to slide slowly down her arm. She felt his warm skin through the thin silk of her sleeve, then his fingers touched her wrist, lightly caressing her pale skin, which was in such strong contrast to his own tanned body, making the very hairs on her flesh prickle and tremble in reaction to him.

'You aren't going away with him!' he said brusquely. 'I like Charles, I've become fond of him, and I realise you're fond of him, too, but you aren't in love with him, Martine, you never have been. For God's sake, the man's a burnt-out case. I'd say that ever since he crashed his car and killed his wife he's only been half alive. There's no vitality in him, and you're a very vital woman. You need a man to light your fire, not put it out.'

'You know nothing about what I need!' she muttered, her lids down, but unable to stop looking at him through her lashes.

'Oh, yes, I do, Martine, you know I do,' he said, his voice deep and hot with excitement, and she began quivering violently, her senses vibrating to the note in his voice.

From across the room she had felt the power of his body; at close quarters it drew her like a magnet, as the moon pulled the tides across the dark face of the globe.

She had a sudden vision of him naked, as he had been that night in Rome; the smooth cool skin of his muscled shoulders, the power of his chest, the way the rough dark hair curled down his body, his slim hips, the bush of black hair curling where his thighs began. A rush of hot desire rose inside her, drowning everything else in her mind.

It seemed an eternity since she had last seen him; he had never been out of her head all that time; she had dreamt about him, fantasised about him, day and night, and now he was here and she could touch him if she wanted to, but she wouldn't let herself be that crazy. She had surrendered to this sensual craving once, and regretted it ever since. She wouldn't do it again.

'Why don't you leave me alone?' she muttered, trying to slide past him, but then his hand closed on her wrist like an iron bracelet and jerked her towards him.

'Don't!' She fell against him, put her hands up to push him away; his arm came round her, making

an unbreakable bar across her back, and her green
eyes grew wide and desperate.

'I don't believe you've slept with Charles,' he said
fiercely. 'You aren't in love with him—we proved
that in Rome, didn't we? If you were in love with
Charles you wouldn't want me!'

'I don't,' she hoarsely said.

'Do I have to prove it all over again?' His eyes
were riveted on her parted, trembling mouth, and
she felt her flesh burn under his stare, stared back
at him like a rabbit at a snake hypnotising it.

'No,' she whispered, terrified.

'But I don't need to prove it, do I?' Bruno said.
'It shows in your face.' He put his head down suddenly, and she gave a strangled cry as she felt his
mouth burn into her throat, making her pulses beat
out of control. 'And I can feel it, here,' he whispered against her skin, and her eyes shut; she felt
her legs give way under her. 'And here,' he said,
his mouth silkily travelling up to kiss the pulse
beating behind her ears. 'And here,' he said, his
head descending again to the open lapels of her
shirt, pushing between them to the pale cleft between her breasts, to track down the wild drumbeat
of yet another pulse.

She gave a helpless cry of passion, her head
falling back, her hands clutching at him to keep her
upright.

'Charles will never make you feel like that,' he
told her, and then lifted his head, and she opened
her eyes to find his dark stare remorselessly ob-
serving what he had done to her, noting her hectic

flush, the dazed brilliance of her eyes, her quick breathing.

Martine despised herself, and almost hated him for being able to reduce her to this slavish level in a moment. Bitterly she threw at him, 'But Charles makes me feel safe...'

There was another charged silence, then his hands bit into her arms and he shook her angrily.

'Safety? Is that what you've convinced yourself you need? Yes, I've no doubt Charles could give you all the security in the world, if it's money you're after, and I suppose that is what you want? Wealth, social position... is that what really turns you on, Martine?'

His harsh, contemptuous tone was like a slap round the face. She couldn't even answer him, she was so insulted.

'No answer?' Bruno snarled. 'Well, I can promise you, you'll never feel safe while I'm around, Martine, whether you marry Charles or not. I'll make sure of that.'

CHAPTER SEVEN

FLYING back from Vienna after Christmas, Martine felt her stomach cramp at the thought of seeing Bruno again. For her, the holiday had been haunted by the memory of the threat in Bruno's face, in his harsh voice, on the day before she and Charles left London.

She should have told him that she had no intention whatever of marrying Charles! But when his black eyes had blazed down at her with that look of contempt she had wanted to hit back at him somehow, anyhow. If he wanted to believe she was pursuing Charles, let him! she had thought, which had been stupid.

She'd known that, a few minutes later, but had been too proud to go after him and tell him the truth. Would he have listened anyway? Probably not.

Her mood shifted again; she scowled out of the plane window at the clouds through which they were descending. If he believed she was capable of marrying Charles for his money, nothing she could have said would have made any difference.

'Aren't you feeling well?' Charles asked, his voice anxious.

She turned, startled. 'What?'

'Your colour keeps coming and going and you're so tense!' He glanced down at the arms of her seat

and she looked down, too, only then realising how
she was gripping them, her knuckles white.

Hurriedly she relaxed her fingers. 'Landing
always makes me nervous,' she lied.

'Nice to get back to London, though,' Charles
said contentedly, stretching in his seat. 'Vienna was
terrific, but I'm always glad to get back to London
and work.'

'Vienna was a dream,' Martine said, closing her
eyes to visualise it. Vienna in the snow was the-
atrical: a chandelier of a city, glittering and faintly
unreal at times, the imperial palaces, the cathedrals
and churches, like forgotten props, discarded
scenery, for this was a city haunted by its Habsburg
past, echoing with dead voices and living music.

Had Charles forgotten how much he'd seemed
to be enjoying himself while he was there?

'I could spend a year here without getting bored,'
he had said as they sat at a table in the window of
a café near the Spanish Riding School, a baroque
hall where the great white thoroughbred Lippizaner
stallions with their uniformed riders performed to
classical Viennese music twice a week during set
times of the year. They had come at the wrong time
of the year, but they had wanted to see the building,
and then they had gone into the café to sip
Einspanner, glasses of coffee which had towering
alps of whipped cream capping them, and had eaten
slices of Sachertorte, a rich chocolate gateau hiding
a layer of delicious apricot jam under the icing.

'You might not get bored, but you'd get fat!'
Martine had said, pushing away her cake, unfin-
ished. 'Gorgeous, but too rich for me. Viennese

cakes must be the best in the world. What are we going to do on our last day here?'

'We haven't had our ride through the Vienna woods yet,' Charles had pointed out. 'Let's do that tomorrow.'

'Yes, I'd love that, it's one of the things I was most looking forward to. I wonder if you can still ride in a sleigh?'

'No doubt at a price,' Charles had said drily. 'The woods will be deep with snow, of course.'

'Oh, wonderful! I'll wear my new red boots, and the cap and mittens I bought at the Christmas fair,' Martine had said.

'Any more shopping to do?'

'No, my suitcase is already packed with presents I'm taking back. I don't have any more room.'

Charles had looked at her wistfully. 'You aren't sorry you came, are you, Martine?'

'Of course not, I've had a wonderful time!'

It was the truth—and yet not quite true. Christmas had been fun, they had given each other presents, enjoyed Christmas lunch Viennese-style, goose stuffed with apples, onions, raisins and nuts, served with red cabbage and potato dumplings; Charles had drunk lots of Austrian beer. They had flung themselves into Christmas like children: pulled crackers, worn paper hats, waved streamers.

After dinner each night they'd waltzed to Strauss on the highly polished parquet floor of the ballroom, enjoyed the floor show, dancers, jugglers, mime artists, musicians, laughed and talked with other guests.

Yet Martine had felt melancholy; she didn't know quite why, perhaps because she kept remembering Bruno's angry eyes and wanting to cry; perhaps because she felt guilty at not having gone home, although her parents had said they understood why she wanted to do something different that year, and hadn't seemed hurt. They had always been self-sufficient, she didn't imagine her absence would spoil their usual quiet Christmas, yet she still felt guilty.

The hotel was exceptionally comfortable, the food excellent, the staff kind, but it was the strangest Christmas she had ever spent. Charles had seemed livelier than he had been for a long time; he threw himself into everything, determined to enjoy himself, so for his sake she was glad she had come. But, in the end, they had not got their ride through the Vienna woods in the snow.

Martine had felt too ill on their last day. The food in Austria was so rich; and since she'd got pregnant any unusual food made her queasy. The only cure was to rest, keep still, and be very careful what she ate and drank, and so she had stayed in the hotel, resting on her bed, all day, while Charles had amused himself taking a last look around the Kunsthistorisches, the Museum of Fine Arts, spending over an hour in the amazing room which held more than half the known works of art of Pieter Breughel the Elder. They had already seen them earlier, but Charles had wanted to see them again. 'Hunters in the Snow' and 'Peasant Wedding' were two of his favourite paintings. He sat in front of them for a long time, he said to her later, worshipping the genius of his favourite painter.

'There's such vibrant, earthy life in every brushstroke Breughel ever painted,' he said, as they landed at Heathrow, skidding slightly on the wet tarmac. 'You know, there was this woman in one canvas, very pregnant; I kept thinking of you. And I thought...you're going to have to tell Bruno about the baby sooner or later, you know, Martine?'

She turned her head to look at him, her face tense. 'I'm not going to! And you'd better not, Charles! I don't want him to know anything about the baby.'

'I understand you're angry with him, but... Martine, I'm sorry, but I have to say this. I think he has the right to know,' Charles said, sounding quite grave. 'I'd want to, if it was my baby.'

'You're not Bruno,' Martine said bitterly. 'You have a strong sense of personal responsibility. He has none at all. And, anyway, I'm the one having this baby, not him. It's nothing to do with him.'

Charles shifted restlessly, looking pugnacious. 'I thought you had more sense than to repeat all that claptrap about the woman being the only one with rights over a baby just because it happens to be carried inside her for nine months. Genetically, half the input of that baby came from Bruno, after all. Surely that gives him some rights? I'm sure he would agree to help you financially, and, even though you earn a very good salary a baby can be expensive, especially if you're going to have a full-time nanny.'

'I wouldn't take his money if I had to beg in the street instead!' she broke out, trembling violently.

Charles looked taken aback.

Martine saw she had shocked him again. Charles, like most men, had a strongly conservative streak; he was easily shocked by unconventional behaviour. She wanted to laugh and cry at the same time, but it was tears that won, aching behind her eyes. 'Charles, I don't walk to talk about this,' she said huskily, blinking the tears away. 'I'm too tired, I just want to get home and go to bed. My head aches, and I can't think straight. Can we leave this discussion until some other time?'

'I'm sorry, was I badgering you?' Charles said, sounding conscience-stricken. 'I won't say another word; why didn't you tell me you were so exhausted? Poor girl, you do look white. If you aren't better on Monday, take some time off. You ought to see your doctor, too, have a check-up— you might be anaemic or something. Isn't that quite common with pregnant women?'

She laughed helplessly. 'Oh, Charles, you're so sweet. Don't worry, my iron intake is fine. I'm sure I'll be back to normal on Monday. Flying always makes me feel tired.'

He dropped her off at her flat an hour after they landed, and she went straight to bed and slept like the dead.

Next morning she drove up to visit her parents and take them their Christmas presents. She did not tell them that she was going to have a baby, and so far there was nothing to betray the fact.

Nevertheless her mother picked up on her weariness and gave her an anxious look.

'Your holiday in Vienna doesn't seem to have done you much good; you seem very pale, love.'

'I'm fine, just tired after the drive up here.'

Her father gave a disapproving grunt. 'You do too much travelling—we keep getting these post-cards from you. Rome one minute, then you're in Germany, now Austria...it's a wonder you don't get giddy, flying around the world all the time. You'll be thirty before you know it, and still not married. And never will be, always going off on your travels! This boss of yours, is he a married man? What does his wife think about him going away with you all the time?'

'His wife was killed in a car crash, Dad,' her mother murmured uneasily. 'You remember, our Martine told us about it. Very sad, poor man. Is he getting over it yet?'

Martine shook her head. 'I doubt if he ever will.'

She left for London again the following afternoon and got back to her flat in a howling blizzard. She was exhausted, shivering violently; she ran a hot bath and stayed in it until the water began to cool, felt quite dizzy as she got out of it, and went to bed at once, with a hot water bottle and several duvets piled on top of her.

In the morning she couldn't get up. She felt feverish, her limbs ached, she had a headache. Not more flu! she thought gloomily, then rang Charles to explain, but he had already rung to say he would not be coming in to work either.

'We must both have the same bug!' she said to his secretary, who sniffed.

'I wonder where you both picked it up, then!' she said with a drop of acid in her voice.

Martine didn't reply, but after she'd rung off she lay in bed thinking grimly. Was there a lot of gossip going round the firm about her and Charles? Nobody had said anything in front of her, but she knew how the staff talked. Neither she nor Charles had mentioned to anyone that they were going on holiday together, but it might somehow have got out. What conclusion would they jump to? The same as Bruno? That she and Charles were having an affair?

She made an angry face. The gossip had to be stopped. But, how was she going to stop it? Maybe she should confide in someone, casually, make sure the truth circulated instead. Her own secretary? Her head hurt too much, she couldn't think clearly; she turned over and went to sleep.

Hours later, she was woken up by somebody ringing the front doorbell. She ignored it. It couldn't be anything important. Then it came again, louder; a sharp, insistent ringing she couldn't ignore.

She yawned, looked at the clock on her bedside table. Just gone midday. She dragged herself out of bed, put on a turquoise-blue velvet dressing-gown over her blue nightdress and wearily made it to the front door, keeping it on the chain as she opened it.

Through the crack Bruno's black eyes flashed over her. 'Oh, you *are* here!'

'Where did you think I'd be? The Sahara?' What was *he* doing here?

'As you and Charles both conveniently rang in to say you were taking sick leave, I did wonder if I'd find you sharing one bed!' he told her with dry sarcasm.

'Oh, go away, I'm too ill to cope with you,' she said, hating him. She tried to shut the door and found his foot in the way.

'Let me in,' he said.

Her green eyes glazed with tears because it made her heart ache just to see him and she was too ill to hide it.

'I'm not that crazy!' she bitterly said. 'Just go away, will you?'

He stared at her, grimly, walked away, and then, before she could shut the door, he came running back, full tilt, hit the door with a tremendous crash, and she felt the thin chain snap. The door swung open and Bruno came with it, almost knocking her off her feet.

As she stumbled backwards Bruno shut the front door behind him with a kick and caught her by the waist, almost in the same movement picking her up and carrying her into her bedroom. He sat down on her tumbled bed with her on his lap, both arms around her.

Her head whirling, she glared up at him. 'Who do you think you are? John Wayne? How dare you smash your way into my flat? Now I shall have to have a new chain fitted! I'll send you the bill. And let go of me, will you?'

He ignored her, pulled open the belt of her dressing-gown and began pushing it off her shoulders.

Her face burning, she slapped his hands away. 'What do you think you're doing? If you think for one moment that I'd let you touch me again, you're out of your skull! Even if you were the last man on earth! I'd rather die. Let go of me!'

He dropped her dressing-gown on the end of the bed, got up, letting her slide on to the bed. 'Get in between the sheets!'

'I'll scream the place down if you lay one finger on me!' she muttered, her head swimming.

'Don't be stupid, woman!' he growled, yanked back the duvets and the top sheet, smoothed down the bottom sheet deftly, as if accustomed to making his own bed, then turned, picked her up, kicking and fighting, and almost threw her down, her head tumbling on to the pillows. Then he pulled the bed-clothes back up over her, and she sagged, feeling too strange to argue any more, closed her eyes, a few weak tears trickling down her face.

'Bully.'

He bent down and talked close to her ear. She felt his warm breath on her lobe and shivered. 'Have you been taking anything? Any medicine? Have you seen a doctor?'

'No,' she said. 'Paracetamol. I don't need anything else. I've just got a touch of flu.'

'What's the name of your doctor?'

Panic streaked through her; her doctor might tell him that she was expecting a baby. She struggled up on one elbow, glaring at him through her tangled auburn hair.

'I don't want a doctor. Will you go away? Leave me alone! All I need is sleep.'

He stared down at her, blackly frowning; then he walked over to the windows and pulled the curtains together, plunging the room into shadow. Collapsing back on to her pillows, Martine watched him walk to the door.

'Goodbye,' she said to his back, and through her half-closed eyes stared hungrily at the long, graceful line of his spine as he moved, the elegant motion of the body under his smoothly tailored suit. Her mouth went dry at the memory. His black hair was dishevelled and windswept; it had looked like that while he was rising and falling above her; she had run her hands into it, clenching fingers in those strands.

She couldn't bear to remember it. Groaning, she shut her eyes.

He went out without a word, a backward look, closing the bedroom door behind him. She listened. Another door closed, sharply. The front door, she thought. He had gone. She shut her eyes, her lashes wet with tears; she wouldn't think about him. She sought refuge in sleep; her last resource.

Her dreams were feverish, troubled; she was perspiring heavily, her temperature must have broken and she was hallucinating. At one point she dreamt that Bruno was there, touching her, taking her nightdress off; she moaned in protest, so hot that it was as if she was on fire. He wiped her sweating face with a cool, damp sponge and she sighed

gratefully. Then his hands gently began to stroke
her body, sponging her breasts, her flat belly, her
thighs. Another sort of heat began to burn in her
and she groaned, putting her hand out, closing her
fingers over his, holding his hand between her
thighs.

'Bruno,' she whispered, shuddering, and heard
his intake of breath.

For a second neither of them moved, and then
he moved her hand aside without a word, began to
pat her skin dry softly. The heat in her subsided.
She felt cooler, her head was clearer. Bruno whispered, 'Go back to sleep now.'

But was she asleep, or dreaming? she thought
dazedly, because it was so real; the desire had been
so piercing she couldn't believe she had dreamt it.
She forced her eyes open and looked around for
him, but he wasn't there. Her bedroom was
shadowy, but empty. She had been hallucinating,
or dreaming, after all.

With a sigh she closed her eyes and went back
to sleep, but now her sleep was deeper, less troubled,
and she no longer sweated the way she had.

The next time she woke up the light had altered;
it was dark. She had no idea what time it was;
wasn't even sure what day it was. A second later
she heard a sound that really woke her up. She
couldn't think what it was at first, then she knew.
Breathing. Someone was breathing. In the room,
near her.

Nerves made her muscles tighten, her pulse-rate
quicken. She carefully flicked her eyes around the
shadowy room, without moving her head; and

tensed as she saw a dark shape just a few feet from her.

Her nerves raw, she knew at once that it was a man, and fear made her sweat. Then she took another hurried, terrified look, and her heart turned over with a crash. Bruno! She looked again, to make certain; but it was him.

She had heard the front door close—how had he got back in here? Or hadn't he gone at all?

She tried to steady her pulse, calm down, before she spoke, but her voice still quivered when she broke out, 'What the hell are you doing in my bedroom?'

He gave an audible start, as if he had been half asleep too; then he leaned forward, switching on the lamp beside her bed. She blinked, half blinded by light, tried to see him through the dazzle. He was sitting in a small armchair he must have brought in here from her sitting-room. He was still wearing his immaculate Savile Row suit, but his shirt collar lay open, his tie was off and she could see the deep tan of his throat, a sprinkling of tiny dark hairs on his upper chest. She swallowed convulsively.

'How do you feel now?' he asked in a voice so casual that it made her mood shoot sky-high with rage.

'Never mind how I feel,' she retorted. 'Tell me why you're still here in my flat! I thought I heard you leave—didn't you go?'

He took a key out of his jacket pocket and laid it on the bedside table.

She stared at it, dumbfounded. 'That's...'

'Your front door key,' he agreed. 'You'd left it lying here, I saw it when I came at lunchtime, so I picked it up and used it to get back in later.'

'You had no right to do that!'

'No,' he admitted without seeming bothered by the admission. 'But I was worried about you.'

She bit her lip, disarmed. 'Oh. Well...that was kind, but, even so...you shouldn't have done it, all the same. I was fine. All I needed was sleep.'

He didn't comment on that, just stood up, dwarfing her, making her throat leap with a wild pulse. 'Can I get you anything? Food? A drink? You should be drinking plenty of liquids.'

There was a jug of lemon barley water and a glass on her bedside table. 'This is fine, and I can manage, thanks,' she said stiffly. 'It was kind of you to be concerned, but I think you should go now.'

'I think you should call a doctor—let me ring him...' he began and she interrupted crossly, face very flushed.

'No, thank you. I can ring him myself if I want him. I'd rather you left now, please.'

'I don't think you're in any condition to look after yourself; this is the second bout of flu you've had this winter. You must be run down, or under stress—isn't that what they say often causes illness?'

She didn't like the hidden insinuation. 'The only stress I'm suffering from is having to put up with you!' she told him coldly.

'That *was* what I meant,' he softly said, and her pulses went haywire again. To cover her confusion she snapped back at him.

'Look, I want to go to the bathroom, so will you get out of my flat?'

'What's the problem, Martine?' he drawled. 'I'm not going to turn dangerous at the sight of you in your nightie getting out of bed. We're way past that, you and I.'

She glared, then knew she could not wait any longer, she had to go to the lavatory. She slid out of bed, picked up her dressing-gown and put it on as she ran out of the room.

It was as she was cleaning her teeth a few moments later, staring at her reflection in the mirror above the sink, that she suddenly noticed her nightdress.

It was not the one she had put on first thing this morning. That had been white lawn, sprigged with blue violas; the one she was wearing now was crisp white cotton striped with yellow.

She stared, rigid with shock, rinsed her mouth and washed her face, dried it, moving like an automaton, her brain racing. She must be going crazy, she must have changed the nightdress during the day, and simply forgotten

She turned to leave the bathroom, and that was when she noticed the wicker laundry basket; the lid was slightly askew and she could see something blue inside. She lifted the lid with a shaky hand. The viola-sprigged nightdress lay on top of the clothes she had worn and discarded yesterday.

She closed her eyes, thinking of her hallucination, or dream: the fever making her sweat, her sheets burning, then Bruno coming, taking off her nightdress, the cool, moist sponge on her body, the clean nightdress going on.

She dropped the lid back on the basket as though it held a snake which might bite her, reached for the door and went out to confront him.

He was in her little kitchen cooking soup in a saucepan. Her nostrils quivered; she realised she was mildly hungry, but she was much too angry to stop and think of that. There was something much more important on her mind.

'You took my clothes off, while I was asleep, you bastard! Didn't you?' she accused hoarsely.

Bruno turned, eyes lazily mocking. 'You mean you only just remembered?'

'I thought I was dreaming,' she began and saw his eyes narrow, gleam.

'You have interesting dreams!' She felt the provoking drift of his eyes down over her body and pulled the lapels of her velvet dressing-gown closer together, but that only made him laugh.

'Look,' he said, 'I found you in a terrible state— your temperature had broken and you were bathed in sweat. You'd kicked your bedclothes off, your nightdress was saturated; the material was so thin it clung to you from your neck to your knees, like a second skin.' He paused, lowered his lashes, looked at her through them teasingly. 'A transparent skin, of course.'

'Oh, shut up, you're deliberately trying to wind me up!' she muttered.

Blandly, he said, 'Well, I couldn't leave you like that, could I? So I found a clean nightie for you, a towel and a sponge, and took care of you.'

'You should have woken me up!'

'I spoke to you, and when I started taking your nightie off to wash you you opened your eyes and looked at me.' His lashes lifted again, she saw his eyes, brilliant, black and hot, like the heart of a slow-burning fire, and trembled. 'Don't pretend you didn't know what I was doing, Martine,' he said huskily. 'You gave me a very tempting invitation...'

Scalding colour poured up her face as she remembered trapping his hand between her thighs, saying his name in a pleading voice. She had wanted him to make love to her, and he knew it. She couldn't bear to look at him.

'You were too ill or I would have had to get in bed with you,' he murmured. 'So I was the perfect gentleman, I let you go back to sleep, and then I sat here, going crazy with frustration.'

'I was hallucinating! Out of my head! I didn't know what I was doing!' she whispered, biting her lip.

'Oh, I think you did,' he whispered, and took a step towards her.

She shot back, agonised by the conflict in her between a wild temptation and a reluctance to get hurt again, throwing up her hands as a frail barrier. 'Don't! I couldn't bear it!'

He stopped dead at the anguish and fear in her voice, staring at her fixedly, his face hardening, darkening.

'That wasn't the impression I got a few hours ago!'

'I told you ... I was out of my head, but now I'm not, and I don't want you to touch me.'

'Wrong wording, Martine,' he bit out, his face grimly contemptuous. 'You want me to touch you, but it's Charles you've decided to marry, isn't it? Your body wants one thing and your head wants another.' His voice thickened, roughened. 'Of course, I could force you to admit how you feel about me...'

She tensed, shaking, going white.

He laughed harshly, watching her with inexorable eyes. 'Oh, don't worry, I'm not going to! I realise it wouldn't make any difference, because I'm not telling you anything you don't know already, and haven't decided cold-bloodedly to ignore. We both knew in Rome, in the street, when we saw those two kids making out in a doorway, didn't we? I envied them like hell and so did you; it must have seemed so simple to them, at their age. They saw each other, wanted each other, took each other— they didn't let anything get in the way of what they desired, not even their own minds! They certainly wouldn't put a barrier up to shut out desire simply because of ambition, or some craving for security!'

'Maybe they wouldn't, but we're not teenagers,' she said quietly. 'We're both adults who know the score where life is concerned. Life isn't simple; and taking what you want without thinking about it can have disastrous consequences.' She took a deep breath, her chin lifted. 'As we're being so frank, I'll admit...you can turn me on.'

His eyes narrowed, brilliant, demanding.

She shook her head at him. 'But you're right, I do prefer to follow the dictates of my head, not my body. The body can betray you; it can lead you into a trap. I know, I've been in love before, and been betrayed.'

His brows jerked together. 'When was that?'

'Never mind; the point is, I learn from my mistakes.'

'Does he work at the bank?'

'Never mind about him...' she said irritably. 'Don't side-track me! He's not relevant.'

'He is to me,' Bruno said tersely. 'If he's one of the reasons why you're so determined to ruin your life, he's relevant.'

'Well, he didn't work at the bank, and you don't know him, but he was rather like you, in some ways.'

Bruno's face tightened.

She sighed. 'I seem to go for a type, and it's the wrong type for me. You are wrong for me, Bruno and I know how any affair I had with you would end in tears; so I'm not starting one. I have other plans for my future, so please, leave me alone from now on, find someone else to play your games with.'

'Your other plans do involve Charles, though, I may take it?' he harshly asked.

She nodded, her face tense and bleak. It was not quite a lie, since she certainly hoped that Charles would be around to run the bank and help her career, and she knew that she dared not tell Bruno the truth. She had to send him away, and she couldn't think of any other method of doing it.

He gave her a long, cold, deadly stare, his mouth twisting. 'Well, then, I won't waste any more of my time on you. I won't say I hope you'll be happy with Charles, because I know you won't be. He isn't the man for you, you're going to ruin his life as well as your own, and I hope you're as miserable as sin, because that's what you deserve.'

He turned on his heel and walked away; she heard the front door slam and the sound reverberated round her flat like the knell of doom.

CHAPTER EIGHT

WINTER seemed to drag on endlessly; January was icy, February it rained almost every day and during those grey, wet days it finally became impossible for Martine to hide the fact that she was going to have a baby.

She had been disguising it with loose tops or baggy sweaters over straight skirts with hidden elasticated waists, but the outline of the body under her loose clothes became all too apparent towards the end of February. By that time she was more than five months pregnant and, physically, feeling much better than she had for a long time. The first four months of her pregnancy had been fraught with sickness; her body hadn't reacted well to its new condition and she had had far too much time off work. Now suddenly she was blooming—skin clear, eyes bright, hair glossy—and was full of driving energy.

The whispers had begun though. First, people fell silent when they saw her, exchanged glances, whispered, covertly studied her changing figure. Martine flushed and tried to pretend not to be aware of the stares, but in the end decided it was time to confide in someone, so she picked Annie, the share analyst who was probably her closest female friend at the bank, and gave her an edited version of the truth.

Annie was a warm-hearted girl; she had a lively personality and men swarmed round her like flies round a honey pot, but she had been let down more than once by a guy she was really keen on. She sympathised at once with Martine's predicament.

'Men can be such rats! He dumped you as soon as he knew you were going to have a baby? Isn't that typical!'

'Well, no, he dumped me before I knew, actually,' Martine felt obliged to explain. Although why she should feel she had to defend Bruno like that she did not know, especially as she hadn't told Annie who the father was and it wouldn't enter Annie's head to suspect Bruno anyway, since Martine and Bruno had never been an item, publicly. Nobody had got an inkling that they had ever been involved with each other.

'Oh? Well, what did he say when you told him?' Annie asked.

'I haven't.'

Annie stared, openmouthed. 'But why not?'

'I don't see him any more; it's over, finished, I don't want him back.' That would make quite sure that nobody ever did suspect Bruno to be the father, she thought, if they believed the man was out of her life.

'I don't blame you, he sounds an absolute beast— but you ought to make him help out with money! I would. After all, it is his baby, too.' Annie's eyes rounded. 'Oh. Is he married? Couldn't he afford to help you because he has kids already?'

Martine almost nodded, then shook her head. 'But that isn't the point, I don't want his money!'

'Well, I jolly well would!' said Annie forthrightly. 'Or aren't you going to keep the baby?'

'Yes, but I can afford to take care of it without help from anybody,' Martine said, and Annie gave her an envious grin.

'On your salary, I suppose you can!' Annie did not earn anywhere near the same amount. 'Will you get a nanny?'

'For the first year, anyway, then I thought I might be able to get an au pair, or something of the sort.'

'Does Mr Redmond know?' Annie always blurted out her first thought; she had a naïve honesty which Martine liked. 'He's so conservative, isn't he? Downright stuffy sometimes! I bet he was shocked.'

'Charles is a darling,' Martine said, resenting the criticism of Charles, mild though it was.

Annie giggled. 'Oh, we all know you adore Charles—in fact a lot of people in the firm have been laying money on it that Charles is the baby's father, and I——' She broke off as someone walked into the room. Annie looked round, started to smile eagerly as she recognised Bruno, who was still her pin-up of the month, then stopped smiling as quickly, meeting a glare like black ice from him which sent her eyes skidding helplessly away.

'Nothing to do, Annie?' he bit out. 'The bank doesn't pay you for sitting around drinking coffee and gossiping.'

She scrambled down from her usual perch on Martine's desk and fled, for once totally wordless.

Martine looked at her computer screen, her mouth ash-dry with apprehension.

Bruno had been away for a fortnight, in Tokyo; this was his first day back and she knew at once that he had heard the gossip about her. She had been dreading this moment for a long time; the moment when Bruno first heard about the baby. Would he guess at once that it was his?

He closed the door and prowled across the room like a caged animal, making her nerve-ends raw, setting her heart thudding.

'Is it his baby?'

The question hit her like whiplash and her head jerked back in shock.

'I don't want to talk about it,' she whispered, her head turned away, her pale profile half veiled by the glowing dark red of her hair, which she was wearing loose these days because she had had it restyled, shorter, easier to do in the mornings. She had changed her whole image, for some reason she couldn't have explained—wearing softer colours, lipsticks, eye-shadow, a very light foundation. It wasn't just her pregnancy that had made her look so different; the change had begun in her mind.

Bruno's black eyes brooded on her. 'You were talking about it to that half-witted blonde just now. Why can't you talk to me?'

'Annie is a friend.'

He was suddenly rigid beside her. Out of the corner of her eye, she saw his hand clench, the knuckles showing white, and flinched, for a second afraid that he was actually going to hit her. The silence stretched between them like barbed wire; she heard him breathing, on his side of the wire;

dragging air into his lungs as if he was only just able to breathe.

'No,' he said at length, bitingly, 'I have no ambition to be one of your friends.'

That hurt. She wanted to yell back at him, but she mustn't let him see that he had hurt her. She managed somehow to keep all expression out of her face, her head held high.

Then the phone rang and she answered it quickly, grateful for the interruption, hoping he would go, but he didn't, he stood by the window, looking out into the chilly February sky, his shoulders back, his hands jammed into his trouser pockets, his black hair sleekly brushed back from his grim face.

The caller was a client, wanting to hear the latest news on a capitalisation scheme they were handling. Martine took her time explaining to him, but she couldn't keep the phone conversation going for ever, and the client finally rang off, thanking her.

She risked a glance at Bruno then and tensed up as she found him watching her with eyes like obsidian, glassy, black, volcanic.

'Did you do it deliberately?'

That question rocked her. 'Deliberately?'

'You know very well what I'm asking—did you get pregnant deliberately?' It seemed to make him even angrier that she was so bewildered. 'What were you trying to do? Force Charles's hand? Make him marry you? Was that your game plan?'

Darkly flushed, she stood up, turned on him, trembling, indignant. 'You've got a horrible mind! I'm not listening to any more of this, get out of here!'

'Not yet,' he said through his teeth. 'I want to know...did it work? Is he going to?'

'Go away!' She put her hands over her ears to shut out the relentless drill of his voice.

He took two strides closer; his hands closed over her wrists and yanked her hands down. The sudden contact sent fever through her veins; she swayed like grass in a high wind. Bruno bent towards her, muttered fiercely, 'He isn't, is he? I can tell from the way you're reacting. He still won't marry you. He may be fond of you, I think he is—he may fancy you, I imagine most men do. But marriage is something else again, and he probably knows why you want to marry him; he's no fool. It wouldn't be a love match, would it? Maybe Charles doesn't want to be married for his money, or for security, and you should have known he wouldn't sit still for this sort of blackmail, either.'

'Blackmail?' she repeated, stunned.

'What else do you call it? You're trying to force his hand and using this baby as a weapon. I call that blackmail, and you should have known it wouldn't work with Charles. You've worked with him for years, you should know him better than that. Charles may be a nice enough guy in private, but he has sabre-toothed tiger in his make-up or he wouldn't have been so successful heading this bank for years. You don't run a big City institution like this one without having predatory instincts.'

'You should know!' she bitterly said.

He gave her a cool look. 'So, if Charles refuses to marry you, what the hell are you going to do?

Will he acknowledge that he's the father, and make some sort of settlement on you and the child?'

'I have no intention of asking my child's father for money! And would you please let go of my wrists? You're hurting!'

He looked down, as if surprised he still held her, then unclenched his hands and let her go.

She looked at her wrists, the faint dark red line around them, where his fingers had gripped.

'I hope you're proud of yourself, leaving marks on me like that!'

'The marks you've left on me won't heal as fast!'

The snarl of the words made her flinch away in shock, feeling as if she had innocently opened the door of a house to find it was on fire when flames leapt out at her.

Bruno's skin had been a dark, angry red; now it was white and icy, like the face of a marble statue, and his eyes looked very black, impossible to fathom.

The silence between them was charged with electricity; she became terrified that he would touch her again, and send her emotional temperature sky-high.

'I told you that you were playing a dangerous game,' he said in a low, harsh voice, making her ears buzz with hypertension. 'I warned you, Martine. Sex is dynamite; you can't treat it with contempt, it's always likely to explode and blow you sky-high. You thought Charles would be easy to handle, as safe as houses—but, you see, you were wrong.'

Angrily she said, 'OK, I was wrong and you were right—there, does that make you feel happier? Is that what you were waiting for me to say? Consider it said. Now take your satisfied ego and get out of my office with it.'

Bruno stared at her, his face taut, then suddenly turned on his heel and strode out, slamming the door behind him; making her windows rattle and a glass on her desk vibrate noisily. Martine burst into tears, covering her face with her hands, put her head down on the desk and sobbed weakly until she managed to choke back her tears and pull herself together.

The next time she saw him Bruno totally ignored her, his eyes icy. He walked past her in the bank as if she were invisible; she felt as if he had slapped her face and had to bite her lip to stop herself betraying the pain she felt.

From then on, that was how it was between them. If nobody else was around he pretended not to see her. If there were others present he spoke to her, politely, coolly, but never quite met her eyes.

Martine kept out of his way as much as possible and fought to keep a calm look on her face whenever she did see him, but the ache inside her deepened day by day.

She was, however, seeing a great deal of Charles, out of working hours. One day every week he spent at a clinic having counselling and some sort of treatment about which he didn't like to talk. Martine had promised she would always be there for him when he needed her during this time. At first his treatment always left him grey and drained, but then he would recover a little; sometimes would take her out to dinner or to a play. It helped him keep his spirits up, especially the night before treatment, when he was obviously frightened and worried.

Gradually as the weeks went by he began to look more like his old self, to have some energy again, but above all to start enjoying life once more.

On a bright spring day in late April Martine went into his office with a pile of letters to discuss with him and he looked round at her with a spontaneous smile, full of warmth.

'Good morning, Martine! You know, being pregnant really suits you—you look lovelier than I've ever seen you.'

She put the letters on his desk, grimacing. 'Thanks, but I feel absolutely huge.'

'How much longer till the baby arrives?'

'It's due in five weeks.'

They both looked down at her bulge indulgently; and as they did she felt the fluttering little kick which kept coming these days, like an internal hiccup.

Charles gave a little gasp. 'I saw that! Your tummy sort of... rippled... what was it?'

'The baby, kicking, silly!' she said, grinning at him.

He gave her an uncertain look. 'Can I... would you mind if I...'

'What?' she asked, laughing.

'Feel it?' he said, a little pink.

She was slightly taken aback, but she was also touched by his fascination at the changes in her body during these months. In his mid-forties, having been married, and no doubt had other relationships too, over the years, Charles was still oddly innocent in some respects. He had missed out on children, didn't seem to know much about the process of having a baby and was constantly asking her questions about it; he had even read a book on it the other week. Sometimes she felt that he was having the baby with her, and she knew that his obvious interest had intensified the belief around the bank that Charles was the father.

'If you want to, of course,' she gently told him, and he gave her a shy smile, then tentatively laid his hand on the bulge under her black and white checked smock, but the baby had lapsed back into somnolence, and nothing happened.

Charles looked disappointed. 'It's stopped.'

'Yes, it only kicks when you don't want it to!'

'I bet it's female!' he teased, then hesitantly added, 'Would I be able to hear its heartbeat?'

Her green eyes smiled with affectionate amusement. 'If you want to listen, go ahead! Be my guest!'

Totally absorbed, he leaned his ear against her, his cheek laid along her tummy, and she looked down at his head, gleaming silver in the spring sunlight, with amusement, a smile curving her mouth.

His secretary had gone out a moment after Martine arrived, leaving his door slightly ajar. A movement in the corridor outside caught Martine's attention, she glanced that way and met the searing flash of black eyes.

Bruno was gone before she could react. White to her hairline, she closed her eyes, fighting not to let Charles see her pain.

'I can hear a sort of rustling noise,' he was saying, his cheek still pressing down against her. 'Like somebody crunching up paper, but rhythmic, too. Do you think that could be the baby's heart?'

She swallowed before she could answer. 'Probably.' Her voice sounded quiet, but surprisingly normal.

'Weren't you tempted, when they did the scan, to let them tell you what sex it was?' asked Charles. 'I would have been; I'm dying to know whether it's a girl or a boy.'

'I prefer to wait.'

'Not long now, it's growing every day,' Charles murmured dreamily. 'I can't wait to see it. I wonder what it will look like? You or Bruno? Will it be dark, or a redhead? Green eyes, or black? I can't wait to find out.'

In the beginning, when he had first known she was going to have a baby, he had once said, 'I won't be here to see it born.'

Now, she noted, with a glow of tears in her eyes he talked with certainty of being here to find out the answers to all his curiosity about the baby. There had been some deep change in Charles over the months of her pregnancy; he had turned again towards life, out from the shadows into the light.

She had a sudden strong instinct that he wasn't going to die. Her heart leapt like a salmon, but she resisted the temptation to tell him. At her suggestion they had not mentioned the word death since they came back from Vienna after Christmas. She had wanted Charles to stop dwelling on it, turn his mind to life; and she still did.

Charles suddenly sat up, leaned back in his chair, fiddled with a gold fountain pen on his desk, and without looking at her said, 'I wish it were my baby, you know. I wish you had married me, given me a right to help you, and the baby. We still could... Martine, I wish you'd change your mind, marry me at once, let me give the baby my name. It would make me very happy. Your baby has given me a reason for living.'

'Oh, Charles,' she said huskily, 'that's the loveliest thing anyone ever said to me, but life itself is the best reason for living.' She put her hand over his on the desk and smiled down at him. 'I have to say no again, but I am touched.'

He sighed. 'I can't persuade you to change your mind?'

'No. Charles, I wouldn't do that to you. Any day you might meet someone special and want to marry again—oh, I know there could never be another Elizabeth, but life is full of surprises. You're much too young to shut the door on love. You'll find it again, when you least expect it. Look at the change in you since Christmas—you look so well these days, you're a different man. You're putting on a little weight, your colour is good and your eyes are bright. What you need now is some outside interests—take up a hobby, painting, pottery, golf... anything to get you involved with people again.'

'Funny you should say that; my therapist has been saying something very similar,' Charles said. 'You aren't in a conspiracy with him, are you?'

She laughed. 'Of course not, it's just common sense.' She hesitated then took the risk of asking, 'When do you have your next series of tests?'

'In a few days. Keep your fingers crossed for me,' he said.

Martine was working in her own office later that day when Bruno walked in with a fat dossier on one of their new clients. He dropped it on her desk with a resounding clunk.

'You asked for that, I gather?'

She looked at the name on the outside of the box file. 'Oh, Klempto; yes. Thanks. It wasn't urgent, if you're still working on it.'

'No, I'm leaving early today,' he said curtly. 'You can send it back to my office when you've finished with it.'

'Of course.' She waited for him to leave, her eyes on the dossier cover, tracing the bold black handwriting she recognised at once as his.

He stood there, restlessly shifting his feet, then said in a tone etched with acid, 'Very touching sight, Charles leaning his head against you like that. I could almost hear the violins. The office grapevine tells me that he's become obsessed with this baby, and whenever I see him he can talk of nothing else; they all believe he's going to crack and marry you before it actually arrives in order to make sure it carries his name. Are they right? Are congratulations in order?'

She looked up at him, her green eyes dark with pain. 'No, they're not.'

His mouth was a hard, white line. 'Too bad,' he said, scarcely moving his lips, and then he was gone.

She sat for a long time staring at nothing, but she had grown accustomed to pain during these long months; she pushed the pain away and concentrated on her work. She would not let him keep hurting her the way he just had. One day she was going to wake up to find she was over him, that he no longer possessed her, body and soul, and she could start forgetting about him. She couldn't wait for the day.

That night as she was on her way home on the Underground, staring blankly into the dark windows through which one saw nothing but the walls of the tunnels, the train suddenly hit something with a tremendous crash and all the lights went out.

Martine was sitting down, but the carriage was full of people strap-hanging. Everyone standing up lurched violently, fell sideways; someone heavy fell on top of her, knocking all the breath out of her. She cried out in pain, heard other people screaming, the scrambling as they tried to get up, panic in the voices around her.

'What happened?'

'What's going on?'

'Did we crash?'

'Why don't they put the lights back on?'

'Got a match, someone? Anyone smoke? Got a lighter?'

Somebody struck a match; in the shadowy flare of it the man who had fallen on her struggled to his feet, muttering, 'Sorry...' and people straightened up, tried to get back to normal, then the match went out.

'I wonder if we'll get going again?' somebody whispered.

'If we don't...if we have to stay here...in this tunnel, in the dark, I shall go crazy,' a girl shakily said.

'Keep calm, Karen,' a boy's voice soothed. 'You aren't hurt; they'll get us out, don't worry. We can walk along the tracks to the nearest station, if the train doesn't start.'

'The rails are live!' she gasped.

'They turn them off if there's been an accident,' she was assured.

People began talking all round the compartment, in the dark, calming each other, reassuring, suggesting what might have happened, what might happen next.

It was fifteen minutes before the guard came along with a torch which he shone around the compartment to check that nobody was seriously injured.

'The train in front of us broke down,' he said. 'There was some sort of failure in the warning system, and we hit the back of the other train, but don't worry, nobody was seriously injured. Luckily, we weren't going fast—we got off lightly. Could have been worse. That's the good news. The bad news is that until they've cleared the previous train of passengers we'll have to stay put. But it shouldn't take long. Keep your spirits up and we'll have you all out of here as soon as humanly possible.'

A babble of voices answered him. One man claimed he had a weak heart, and had to be got out at once; someone else was feeling claustrophobic; a woman was sobbing noisily, begging to be allowed to get out at once.

'I hate the dark, I hate it, please, please, let me out of here . . .' she said.

The guard made soothing noises to them all, but could only repeat, 'We'll get you out as soon as humanly possible, I promise.'

Martine didn't say anything. She was in too much pain. Sweat dewed her face, and she was tense and shaking. Ever since the other passenger had fallen on her so heavily there had been a grinding pain in the small of her back. She had never felt it before, but she had read about it, she knew what it was.

The shock of the accident had sent her into premature labour. She had no way of knowing how quickly the process would move, and she was trapped here, without any medical help, in the hot, dark, overcrowded compartment where air was going to run short before too long.

I could lose my baby, she thought, biting her lips as another hard pain hit her. If I don't get help, everything might go wrong with the birth. When she'd first known she was pregnant she had been appalled, she had longed bitterly to turn back the clock, erase the baby from existence.

Now the thought of losing it was agonising.

CHAPTER NINE

THEY got her out of there two hours later, the longest two hours of her life. It was a nightmare trip along the tunnel to the station platform; there wasn't room for a stretcher for most of the way, and she had to walk, pausing every now and then as another pain started. An ambulance man was walking close behind her, encouraging her. 'Not far now, love. Keep going, we're nearly there.'

She didn't answer; she was too busy concentrating on riding the waves of pain; and even when the tunnel widened out and the ambulance men insisted on carrying her on a stretcher it was an uncomfortable ride, in the dark.

At one point she saw tiny points of light in a crevice in the dirt-grimed wall; little red eyes watching her. She screamed, and the ambulancemen stopped dead, peering at her through the half-gloom of the torches fixed on their safety helmets.

'Oh, my God, don't say it's coming!' one said, sounding panic-stricken.

'What is it, love?' said the older man, bending down to her.

'A...rat...I saw a r...rat...' Martine quavered, and there was a silence, then they laughed, half relieved, half disgusted.

'These tunnels are overrun with them; don't worry, they won't hurt you.'

She lay down again, closing her eyes, and minutes later they were in the next station and she was being carried up in a lift to the waiting ambulance.

Martine was admitted to the maternity wing of the hospital closest to her home an hour later, after she had been examined by a young registrar who said she was definitely in labour.

'If you had got here sooner, we might have been able to stop the pains, but I think it's gone too far,' he told her. 'Luckily we have an empty bed.'

She was given a hospital nightgown. 'Do you want to make a phone call? Tell someone you are in here? Make arrangements for a few things to be brought in later?' the ward sister asked, shrewdly noting the absence of a wedding-ring on her hand.

Martine flushed. 'I would like to make a call,' she stiffly said.

'Nurse will bring you a portable telephone.' Sister rustled away down the ward and the young nurse rushed off to obey her.

Charles was at home, luckily. Her news sent him into a tizzy. 'It's very early, is that a bad sign? What are they doing about it? What on earth made it start so early? I'll get a specialist to see you . . . you must have the best treatment . . . a private room, a consultant . . .'

'I'm fine where I am, I'm having the best of treatment, I don't want to be moved,' Martine said, impatiently because she knew another pain would start in a minute. 'Charles, listen, I haven't got much time . . . I'll need a few things from my flat. I'd already packed a case; they tell you to do that in advance. But it's in my flat. Do you think you can get it for me and bring it over here tomorrow?'

'Tomorrow nothing,' Charles said. 'I'm coming now. I want to be in on this. I've got a stake in this baby.'

She smiled faintly, didn't argue. 'It would be nice to have some company, although I don't know if they'll let you stay long.'

'Let them try and get me out!' Charles said belligerently. 'Now, how am I to get into your flat, that is the question.'

'Well, the girl who lives next door to me has got a spare key to my flat—she often takes in parcels and so on for me. Get her to come in with you and find the case—it's in my bedroom in the bottom of the wardrobe. Oh, and Charles, I'd like a few books to read—I have one on my bedside table that I'd like, and there's a bag of knitting on a table somewhere.'

'I'll find them all,' Charles promised. 'See you soon, don't have it until I get there.'

By the time he got there she had been in labour for over five hours and was beginning to tire. Charles was very excited; his eyes shone as he bent to kiss her.

'I talked to that doctor out there, the girl with the run in her stockings . . . she looks very young to be a doctor and bring babies into the world, don't you think so?'

Breathing rhythmically, Martine couldn't stop to answer him, so Charles plunged on, 'Anyway, she said you're doing fine and everything is OK, except that the baby is premature, but not dangerously so, and we're not to worry.'

'Who's worried?' Martine said, relaxing again as the pains stopped. 'Thanks for coming, Charles. Did you find my suitcase? The other things?'

'Everything,' he assured her. 'Your friend next door sent her love; she would have come too, but she's on night duty this week, she said to tell you.'

Martine nodded. 'I know.'

Charles gave her case to the nurse who put it away for the moment; he put some books and a Walkman with headphones and a few tapes into the locker beside her bed, then looked around the little room curiously.

'Is this where you'll have it?'

'No, they'll move me when I'm about to give birth,' she said, then clutched at his hand as another pang came.

Charles sat down beside the bed, holding her fingers tightly. He had discussed her antenatal exercises with her countless times over the past few months and was fascinated now by the real thing, although she caught a flicker of nervous apprehension in his eyes.

'Is it very painful, Martine?'

'I can bear it,' she said breathlessly, laughing, and he bent to kiss her cheek.

'You're so brave.'

A nurse starchily crackled into the room, paused, said rather tartly, 'You've got another visitor wanting to come in—do you want to see him?'

'Him?' Martine repeated, and had a flash of premonition. She looked accusingly at Charles. 'Did you tell Bruno?'

His face was startled but showed no sign of confusion or guilt. 'No, of course not! I didn't tell anyone except your next-door neighbour.'

Martine was in panic. 'Tell him to go away,' she said to the nurse, who turned to go.

'Wait a minute, Nurse,' Charles said. 'What does this man look like?' And then, aside, to Martine, added, 'It could be your father, after all!'

'Can't be,' said the nurse drily. 'He's not old enough. In his thirties, I'd say, tall, dark and sexy.'

Charles looked at Martine. 'It's Bruno, all right.'

'Tell him to go away,' Martine said, the nurse went out and then another pain hit, the strongest so far, and Martine had no time to think about Bruno. She gripped Charles's hand and he watched her anxiously.

A moment later she slackened again, Charles lent over her and wiped her perspiring face with a witch-hazel-drenched pad, from the tin of them which, in anticipation, she had packed in her suitcase.

'Charles, you're such a darling,' she whispered, smiling up at him.

At that moment loud voices made them both stiffen; the door slammed open and Bruno burst into the room, the nurse hanging on to his arm but unable to stop him any more than she could have halted a stampeding elephant.

'Do you want me to call Security?' she was yelling.

Bruno stopped at the bottom of the bed and looked at Martine, his black eyes fixed and grim in his pale face.

'They'll have to bring an army to throw me out of here before I'm ready to go!' he threatened.

Martine saw faces behind them, people in the outer ward, staring, all ears.

She couldn't bear a scene, not now. Wearily, she told the nurse: 'He might as well stay for a moment or two, it's OK.'

The nurse gave her an old-fashioned look. 'Well, make up your mind! And I hope one of them is the father, because our rule book says only one father to a bed.'

She stamped out and Bruno shut the door on the curious faces.

Charles got up and confronted Bruno. 'What on earth do you think you're doing? How did you find out she was here?'

Bruno gave him a deadly look, every bone in his face locked in bitter hostility. 'I wanted to talk to her so I went to her flat, I ran into her next-door neighbour on her way to work, and she told me Martine had gone into premature labour and that you had come for some things for her.'

'Yes, I did,' Charles said, frowning. 'Look, Bruno, you heard Martine—she doesn't want you here. I'm looking after her...'

'I know all about the way you've looked after her!' Bruno snarled and hit him.

Martine choked off an instinctive scream as Charles reeled backwards across the room and fell on to the end of her bed.

'Oh, my God,' she moaned, sitting up and scrambling towards him along the bed. 'Charles ... You could kill him, hitting him like that ... darling Charles ...'

Bruno caught her shoulders and heaved her up towards him. 'You don't love him, you love me, however much you may wish you didn't,' he shouted at her, and as she looked at him, her auburn hair tangled and damp around her face, he groaned out, 'And I'm out of my mind over you, can't you see that? It's getting worse every day. I'm dying for you, Martine, I can't bear it any more—don't waste your life on a selfish swine who doesn't love you enough to marry you!'

'As it happens, I did ask her to marry me,' Charles said thickly, sitting up and massaging his jaw with a rueful expression on his face.

Bruno went white. He looked down into Martine's face, she heard the harsh drag of his breathing.

'And you accepted,' he said, rather than asked, then swallowed, and she saw his throat move convulsively.

'No, she turned me down flat,' Charles answered for her. 'Every time I propose she turns me down.'

Bruno's black eyes flashed to him, then back to Martine. 'What? I don't understand ...'

She clenched up as the pain came again, stabbing, agonising; and Charles hurriedly pushed Bruno aside and came to help her to lie down, soothingly murmuring, 'You've forgotten your breathing, darling... breathe... count...'

The two men watched her raggedly breathing then the breathing slowing as the pain passed.

'But the baby,' Bruno said curtly. 'It's yours; she must have slept with you. Why would she do that and refuse to marry you?'

'No,' Charles said, giving him a dry look. 'I have never slept with Martine.'

'You haven't?' Bruno looked blankly at him.

'No, and the baby isn't mine.'

'It isn't?' Bruno seemed to be having difficulty understanding what Charles was telling him. Charles gave him a wryly amused look.

'No, it isn't; I wish it were.'

'But... if it isn't your baby, why did you ask her to marry you?'

Martine answered that. 'Because he was sorry for me, when he found out I was going to have this baby and had no father for it!'

Charles smiled down at her. 'And because I want this baby too,' he said. 'Having lived through this pregnancy with you right up till now, I feel as if I am the father.'

Bruno's face was rigid, his eyes riveted on Martine's face. 'If he's not the father... I am,' he said, intently watching the expression of her brilliant green eyes. 'I am, aren't I? That night in

Rome . . . but I was so careful! How could you have got pregnant?'

'*I* don't know! Obviously something went wrong; all I know is I ended up having a baby and I didn't sleep with any other man!'

'Why on earth didn't you tell me?' he demanded. 'Why let me think it was his? How could you do that? I don't understand you at all.'

'No, you don't,' she muttered. 'You were the one who decided Charles was the father . . . you were the one who kept insisting that I wanted to marry Charles . . . you wouldn't listen when I told you I didn't . . . you wanted to think the worst of me. I have my pride! I gave up trying to convince you and just let you think whatever you liked.'

His voice roughened by feeling, he whispered, 'You've tortured me all these months, put me into a hell of jealousy and misery, all out of pride!'

Her green eyes darkened. 'Do you think I was rapturously happy?' she said, and then another pain arrived and she stopped talking while she rode it.

'Here,' Charles told Bruno quietly, 'sit down on my chair, hold her hand, help her do her breathing, but stop shouting at her—she's in no fit state to go through an emotional scene just now, can't you see that? You can fight this out after your baby has been born.'

Bruno didn't even look at him, just slid into the chair and gripped Martine's hand.

A moment later when she shifted her head on the pillow, sighing in relief, she saw that Charles had gone and she was alone with Bruno.

Their eyes met, hers wavered, her lashes flicking down against her cheek, then she risked another look at him. 'I'm sorry, Bruno,' she whispered, aching with love.

He lifted her hand, his lips opened hotly against her palm and she trembled as she felt the intensity of the lingering kiss.

'I'm sorry, too,' he said huskily. 'I don't understand you, but I'm desperately in love with you. Don't ever send me away again.'

Their baby was born two hours later, and Bruno was with her throughout the birth, gowned and gloved, like one of the nurses; it was Bruno who laid their daughter on her breast, smiling as Martine gently touched the baby's damp black hair.

'What are you going to call her?' asked Charles two days later.

'Roma,' Martine said, laughing.

'You're kidding?'

She shook her head. 'I think it suits her; she has a distinct Roman nose.'

'Rubbish, poor baby,' said Charles, horrified. 'She's beautiful.'

'You should have seen her five minutes after she arrived—she was all wrinkles, red as a beetroot, and screaming her head off!'

'She looked gorgeous, I saw her as they wheeled her off to the nursery,' Charles said, indignantly, passing her grapes he had carefully peeled for her from a bowl beside her bed.

Martine did a double-take. 'You stayed until then?'

'I sat in the waiting-room with a pile of magazines and an endless supply of ghastly hospital tea to get me through it,' he said, grinning.

She was touched. 'Oh, Charles, that's so sweet . . . you should have gone home and rung up later to find out.'

'I wanted to be here, I wanted to see her arrive in this world,' he said. 'I am still going to be godfather, aren't I? You won't let Bruno change your mind.'

'He wouldn't try,' she said, and Charles gave her a dry look.

'He's so jealous he can hardly bear to look at me.'

She smiled secretly. 'Not any more, not now he realises he was wrong about us!'

Charles didn't look convinced. 'Are you going to marry him, Martine?'

'If he asks me,' she said, knowing he would— and that she was going to grab him with both hands.

Charles gave a gloomy sigh. 'I'm afraid he'll go back to Switzerland and take you and the baby with you, just to get you both away from me.'

'I didn't get the impression he wanted to leave the bank,' she said, startled. 'He loves living in London.'

Charles sighed. 'He's the type who'll want you to give up your job and settle down as a housewife and mother.'

She contemplated that. 'I think I would like to take a few months off, just while Roma is so small,' she tentatively said. 'I can get a nanny later and come back to work, if you want me back, that is.'

'Of course I want you back,' he said, as the door opened and Bruno walked into her room, stopping dead as he saw Charles, who gave him a defiant look. 'I was just going,' he said, getting up.

Bruno held the door open, face dangerous, full of narrow-eyed warning as he stared at Charles. Martine could have hit him.

Charles bent and kissed Martine's nose, pretending to be unaware of the menace behind his back. 'Give my goddaughter a kiss for me . . . oh, and tell her my latest test was very encouraging; they say there's been a striking improvement.'

Martine looked up, eyes glistening with tears. 'Oh, Charles, I'm so glad!' She put her arms round him and hugged him; he held her tightly for a moment, and she said, 'Come again, soon, tell me all about it next time.'

'Wild horses wouldn't keep me away,' he said, meaning that Bruno wouldn't.

Closing the door behind him Bruno asked Martine, 'What test? Improvement in what?'

She told him and Bruno drew a shocked and shaken breath. 'No! My God, no wonder he's looked so terrible at times. That explains a lot. Poor guy.' He frowned, staring at nothing. 'I wish I hadn't hit him. I might have hurt him badly. Why on earth didn't you tell me?'

'He didn't want anyone to know!'

Bruno nodded, mouth a white line. 'Do you think these treatments are genuinely having some effect? Might he recover completely?'

'I'm keeping my fingers crossed,' Martine said 'And, you know, I'm really hopeful.'

Bruno sat down on the edge of the bed beside her. 'It must have been very hard to refuse to marry him, after he'd told you he was going to die soon. You must have felt very guilty about that.'

She nodded, sighing. 'If he had said he loved me, I might have agreed, but we both knew there was nothing like that between us. We were friends, good friends, as close as brother and sister, I think. The only reason he proposed was so that the baby could inherit his estate, and I couldn't possibly marry him for a reason like that.' She gave him a sideways look. 'I know you thought I was chasing him for his money, but then you have a pretty cynical view of women.'

'Based on some I've known,' he said, grimacing. 'I can think of quite a few women I've met who were ready to marry for money.'

'Not me,' she crossly said. 'I'm not mercenary, even though you kept accusing me of it!'

'You deliberately let me think the worst,' he reminded her. 'You did a good job of fooling me, too. I was so jealous of Charles it's a wonder to me I managed to stop myself killing him.' He groaned. 'The worst of it is, I still am. You may have refused to marry him, you may never have been his lover, but the two of you are very close and he is obviously obsessed with the baby.'

She smiled tenderly. 'Yes, isn't he? I'm glad, because it was an obsession that helped him fight this tumour. In fact, I think the baby saved his life—as it grew inside me, I think the tumour shrank; the baby gave Charles a reason for staying alive.'

Bruno was frowning. 'Yet it isn't his—that's odd, isn't it?'

'Don't you believe me?' Martine felt sick at the prospect of dealing with this jealousy of his for ever, but Bruno at once shook his head.

'Of course I believe you, but I can't quite see why the baby should be so important in this.'

'I don't quite know why, either; but it worked that way, Bruno. Thinking about the baby stopped him brooding on the fact that he was driving when he had that crash and killed his wife, and that was what he needed. He was almost willing himself to die; he had to start willing himself to live. Focusing on my baby did that for him. The baby was a new life; it opened the future up for him again.'

Bruno watched her intently. 'What about us? Do we have a future, Martine?'

She took a deep breath, met his dark eyes, her own passionate, shy. 'I love you, Bruno,' she whispered, 'if that is what you're asking.'

'I was asking you to marry me,' he said in a low, husky voice. 'I already know you love me—that was what drove me crazy all through those months, knowing that you were mine, and yet having you refuse to let me near you.'

'I told you, I got badly hurt a few years ago, and I didn't want to risk getting involved again. The morning after we made love, in Rome, I woke up to find you gone...' Her voice broke and she closed her eyes, fighting remembered pain. 'Why did you do that? Why did you go, leaving just that curt note?'

He groaned. 'I wanted to write words that would burn the paper, but I didn't know how you would react to reading how I really felt. I sat there for minutes with a head full of passion, and in the end I just scribbled a brief note and crept out. I didn't want to wake you, you were sleeping so peacefully, but I couldn't stay with you in case somebody saw me in your room. I didn't want a lot of gossip about us spreading around the conference.'

She bit her lip, incredulous. 'But you were so cold when I came down to breakfast! You looked at me with total indifference.'

'That wasn't indifference, or coldness,' he said hoarsely. 'I was shaking like a leaf. I'd been there for half an hour, waiting for you, on tenterhooks, wondering how you would look at me, wondering what you would say...and then you walked in looking like an ice goddess, with that touch-me-not expression on your face, and I felt my insides cave in! The only way I could hide how I felt was to put on a mask, act offhand, pretend I didn't care.'

They stared at each other in silence, then Martine whispered, 'We've both been stupid.'

'Stupid doesn't cover it,' Bruno said. 'All these months, when I've been dying for you... If only you had given me a sign, the tiniest glimmer of hope, but every time I came near you you acted as if I was Public Enemy Number One.'

'I'm sorry, Bruno,' she huskily said. 'I didn't mean to hurt you...' Then she broke off, laughing unsteadily. 'That's a lie. I did want to hurt you; because you had hurt me so badly. I just didn't realise I had the power to hurt you.'

Bruno curved a hand around her flushed cheek, staring fixedly into her green eyes, moving nearer. 'You have the power to make my life a living hell,' he whispered. 'I'm so crazy about you; you've no idea what you've been doing to me in the past few months. I've lost a lot of sleep over you, and had some pretty hectic dreams.'

She felt her colour heat. 'So have I,' she whispered, her lashes falling over eyes full of confusion.

Bruno moved even nearer, and at that moment the nurse knocked on the door and came in with the baby cradled in her arms.

'Feeding time,' she announced. 'Are you ready for her, Mum?' She gave Bruno a sharp look. 'Not on the bed, please, Dad. We don't like that on our wards.'

Bruno got up and walked over to the window, stared out, with his back to them as the nurse helped Martine prepare to feed the baby. Once the little mouth was attached to one nipple the nurse marched out again. As soon as the door had shut Bruno came back to the bed and sat down again, in the same position, watching with fascination as his baby daughter took her meal.

'She's greedy, isn't she?'

'Little pig,' Martine fondly said, looking down at the round dark head absorbedly attacking her. The baby's small hand smacked rhythmically on Martine's warm, white breast while she sucked, and when Martine detached her after the requisite time and transferred her to the other breast the baby began at once to shriek, enraged at being taken away. She only shut up as the other nipple went into her mouth.

'I wonder what it tastes like,' Bruno said huskily.

Martine glanced up at the note in his voice, a new sensation beginning inside her.

Bruno slowly leaned forward; his eyes closing, he took her free nipple into his mouth softly and began to suck, a hand clasping her warm breast, stroking it seductively, coaxing the milk to flow again.

Martine drew a shaken breath, her face burning. 'The nurse will be back any minute, Bruno,' she muttered; yet the feel of his mouth around her nipple, the needle-like flow of the milk, was erotic, sensuous, and she didn't want him to stop. Her hand went out to stroke his warm, sleek hair, her skin prickling with awareness of him.

When he finally lifted his face, looking at her with languorous, passionate eyes, she felt the answering stab of desire deep inside her.

'How long do you go on breast-feeding for?' he whispered, still stroking her breast with one hand.

'Months,' she said.

'Good,' Bruno whispered and she couldn't help laughing, yet at the same time it sent a quiver of arousal through her.

'You're wicked,' she said.

He looked at her through half-closed eyes. 'You have no idea how wicked I can get, given half a chance. Martine, as soon as we can arrange it, we must get married, you must give up your flat and come to live with me, you and our baby. I don't want to miss another moment with you, either of you. Charles, damn him, stole months of our life together.'

She frowned. 'Don't be jealous of Charles.'

'I am jealous of Charles, I want you all to myself.'

'If he were my brother, would you be jealous?'

'He isn't your brother.'

'Not by blood, but in every other sense of the word. I love Charles, in a totally different way. I don't want him, he doesn't turn me on—but I am as fond of him as if he was my brother, and I don't want you to be jealous.'

He looked at her, his mouth crooked. 'I'll keep telling myself he's your brother-figure, but I warn you, Martine, I'm the possessive type. You're mine.'

'Body and soul,' she said, her eyes burning and intense.

She heard the fierce intake of his breath, then he said, 'Just make sure Charles understands that.'

'He understands,' she said, as the nurse arrived to take their baby away again.

She gave Bruno an affronted look. 'You're back on that bed again, Mr Falcucci. I hope I'm not going to have trouble with you. Now, sit on a chair, like everybody else, or leave my ward!'

Bruno sat on a chair until she had left and Martine's open-fronted nightdress had been buttoned up again, then as soon as the door was shut he slid over on to the bed and took her into his arms.

'Will she be back or can we have five uninterrupted minutes alone?' he asked her, his mouth moving against the smooth skin of her long neck.

'They never leave you alone for a whole five minutes!' groaned Martine. 'Bruno! Don't do that.'

His hands were busy, hurriedly undoing her nightgown again, freeing her breasts and stroking them, his fingers trembling slightly. He held her shoulders, pushed her gently backwards on to her pillows, coming down with her, lying half on top of her, his mouth searching for her breast.

She pushed his black head away, laughing huskily. 'No, Bruno—you can't, not here...' Yet she felt the drowning bliss of sensual pleasure even while she tried to stop him; he was making all her dreams come true, but this was not the time.

They both heard the door-handle turn. Bruno shot up and was on his feet before the door began to open. Martine feverishly did up her nightie again, pulling the sheet up to her shoulders.

'Time for Doctor's round, Mr Falcucci,' the ward sister said, looking suspiciously around the room as if picking up unwelcome vibrations from them both. Desire clouded the air with musky perfume. Sister did not like the scent of it, and her nostrils quivered. 'I'm afraid you'll have to go.' She walked over to the door and held it open pointedly.

Bruno came over to kiss Martine goodbye, and took the chance to whisper, 'Get out of this place as soon as you can and come home, my darling. We have a lot of lost time to make up for.'

HARLEQUIN ◆ PRESENTS®

Can you bear the heat!

Our sizzling series of the hottest stories continues....

They're

Coming next month:

Dangerous Alliance by Helen Bianchin
Harlequin Presents #1741

"Is the idea of marriage to me so unacceptable?"

If Dimitri Kostakidas had asked Leanne that question years
ago when she was an impressionable girl who fancied herself
in love with him, the answer might have been a different
one. Now she would do anything rather than share Dimitri's
bed. But there was no choice in the matter and no escape
from the future he had mapped out for her....

Available in May wherever Harlequin books are sold.

HARLEQUIN®

PRESENTS
RELUCTANT BRIDEGROOMS

Two beautiful brides, two unforgettable romances...
two men running for their lives....

My Lady Love, by Paula Marshall, introduces
Charles, Viscount Halstead, who lost his memory
and found himself employed as a stableboy by the
untouchable Nell Tallboys, Countess Malplaquet.
But Nell didn't consider Charles untouchable—
not at all!

Darling Amazon, by Sylvia Andrew, is the story of
a spurious engagement between Julia Marchant
and Hugo, marquess of Rostherne—an engagement
that gets out of hand and just may lead Hugo to
the altar after all!

Enjoy two madcap Regency weddings this May,
wherever Harlequin books are sold.

HARLEQUIN 💎 PRESENTS®

We're not keeping it to ourselves!
Secrets...
**The exciting collection of intriguing, sensual stories
from Harlequin Presents**

Trail of Love by Amanda Browning

Harlequin Presents #1742

Kay Napier was a happy, intelligent young woman who had
been brought up in a loving home. Then lightning struck.
The first bolt came in the disturbingly attractive shape of
Ben Radford. The second was a challenge to her very identity.
It was unsettling to discover that she wasn't who she thought
she was. But nothing as unnerving as finding that Ben wanted
her body, but not her love. And to prove that, Ben intended to
marry someone else....

Available in May wherever Harlequin books are sold.

HARLEQUIN®

An affair...with her own husband? Laura and Dirk had been separated but, all of a sudden, he was back in her life and pursuing her. Laura couldn't forget that she had been unable to conceive Dirk's child, which meant there could be no long-term future for them—so why was she still tempted to accept his simply *outrageous* proposal!

Nell was wary of men, until she met Ben Rigby and found herself longing for something more. But she was afraid. Her child—her lost child, whom she'd never had the chance to see—shared the same birthday as Ben's adopted son...was Fate being cruel or kind?

Harlequin invites you to the most
romantic wedding of the season.

Rope the cowboy of your dreams in
Marry Me, Cowboy!

A collection of 4 brand-new stories,
celebrating weddings, written by:

New York Times bestselling author

JANET DAILEY

and favorite authors

Margaret Way
Anne McAllister
Susan Fox

Be sure not to miss Marry Me, Cowboy!
coming this April

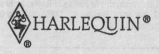

If you are looking for more titles by

CHARLOTTE LAMB

Don't miss these fabulous stories by one of
Harlequin's great authors:

Harlequin Presents®

#11370	DARK PURSUIT	$2.75	☐
#11467	HEART ON FIRE	$2.89	☐
#11480	SHOTGUN WEDDING	$2.89	☐
#11560	SLEEPING PARTNERS	$2.99	☐
#11584	FORBIDDEN FRUIT	$2.99	☐
#11618	DREAMING	$2.99	☐
#11706	GUILTY LOVE	$2.99 U.S.	☐
		$3.50 CAN.	☐
#11720	VAMPIRE LOVER	$3.25 U.S.	☐
		$3.75 CAN.	☐

The following titles are part of the Barbary Wharf series

#11498	BESIEGED	$2.89	☐
#11509	BATTLE FOR POSSESSION	$2.89	☐
#11530	A SWEET ADDICTION	$2.89	☐

(limited quantities available on certain titles)

TOTAL AMOUNT	$
POSTAGE & HANDLING	$
($1.00 for one book, 50¢ for each additional)	
APPLICABLE TAXES*	$_____
TOTAL PAYABLE	$_____
(check or money order—please do not send cash)	

To order, complete this form and send it, along with a check or money order
for the total above, payable to Harlequin Books, to: **In the U.S.:** 3010 Walden
Avenue, P.O. Box 9047, Buffalo, NY 14269-9047; **In Canada:** P.O. Box 613,
Fort Erie, Ontario, L2A 5X3.

Name: _____

Address: _____ City: _____

State/Prov.: _____ Zip/Postal Code: _____

*New York residents remit applicable sales taxes.
Canadian residents remit applicable GST and provincial taxes. HCLBACK4

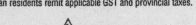

HARLEQUIN®